From the Lady Blade Series:

I0531372

Before the Blade

by

Catherine Thrush

CONTENTS

ACKNOWLEDGEMENTS

Special thanks to Martha, Paulette, and Alan for their patience and their sage advice on my stories.

MY BRAVE GIRL

Salerno
June 8th, 1700

Thurio DiCesare, the famous fencing maestro, felt his heart beat a staccato rhythm as he hurried toward his mother's house. Chaos filled the narrow, cobbled streets packed with horse-drawn carts. He dodged between men and women running in and out of houses, piling wagons with belongings. Children wailed. Carriage drivers cursed as they tried to squeeze their neatly appointed carriages between laden carts and wagons and became wedged, bringing traffic to a standstill. Voices rose. Fist fights broke out.

Fools, thought Thurio. *If they left their belongings and fled, they might stand a chance.*

He turned a corner and entered the slate-blue door of a gray stone house. He called out as he rushed up a staircase two steps at a time. "Mary! Mother! Where are you two?"

Two women appeared at the top of the stairs, their faces pale. Mother wore a navy-blue dress, along with gray hair so tidy as to be almost severe. Her tiny frame leaned on a carved-wood cane. "What has gotten into them?" she asked. "The entire town is in the streets!"

Thurio reached his wife Mary and took her in his arms, relieved that she and their unborn child were safe for the moment. He buried his dark face in her deep copper-colored hair and breathed in her floral scent. He felt her heart race, until she pressed away and looked up at him with spring green eyes. Her dusty green dress and silver stomacher made her eyes even deeper green.

"What is it this time, my love," she said with a smile. "Is the world ending yet again?"

He heard bravado in her light tone, but the narrowing of her eyes told him she was frightened. Something about the English accent to her Italian words reassured him as nothing else could.

"Barbary corsairs," said Thurio, moving past them into the bedroom. "They've raided Amalfi and are headed this way."

"Holy Mary, Mother of God," mumbled Mother.

"Slavers," hissed Mary, putting protective hands around her swollen belly.

The corsairs were pirates out of Algiers and Tunis. They raided in fleets of ships, ravaging the coast, attacking villages, and rounding up townsfolk to sell into slavery across the Ottoman Empire. Towns, villages, whole cities had been emptied of citizens to feed the slave trade over the last centuries. Few victims ever returned.

Thurio knew without looking that his mother made hurried signs of the cross. He glanced up from the drawer that he ransacked for valuables.

Mary leaned against the door frame, a hand supporting her eight-month pregnant belly. "What do we do?" she asked. "Should we head into the hills?"

Salerno nestled between steep hills and the harbor. Few roads led out of town, and Thurio knew from experience that the fleeing citizens and their carts and wagons would clog and block the roads in their panic. The three of them might have headed overland and climbed into the hills to hide, but Mother's fall four months ago had broken her hip. She was healing, but slowly. There was no way she could make the climb.

The Maestro ripped open another drawer, piling jewelry on top of the bureau.

"I've arranged passage aboard a ship." He hated sea travel but had no choice. "I pray God we're in time. Captain Sabatini promised to wait for us." *He has his own family to worry about,* he added to himself. *He may still leave without us.*

"I'll pack my things," said Mary.

"No," said Thurio. "There's no time. Take this jewelry, I'll get my sword and pistols. Then we must go."

———————

They picked their way through the panicking townsfolk and their horses and carts. Mother moved slowly, and groaned in pain when someone bumped into her, so Thurio lifted her in his arms, carrying her. She felt like nothing, so frail and delicate. She'd always been a small woman, but the last few years she had shrunk to nearly nothing. Though Thurio smiled, thinking her spirit had not shrunk in the least.

Mary hurried along with a hand tucked inside Thurio's elbow. He glanced at her, and she gave him an encouraging smile. *My brave girl.*

He remembered the day they met.

In those days he traveled across Europe offering his sword arm to whatever cause paid the best. He had been fighting with the Williamites in the battle near the village of Aughrim. He'd taken a musket ball to the thigh and a slash to his side and sat panting and bleeding in a rutted road with his back to the hedgerow. She had appeared in the evening light with battle still raging. She wore a knife at her side and a healer's bag over her shoulder.

Despite the spattered blood, she was beautiful. Her hair shone in the setting sun and swirled about her, torn loose from its binding. "My little Paprika" he would come to call her, teasing her about the color of her hair. Her green eyes had blazed with intelligence and concern as she looked at his wounds. And when she smiled to reassure him he would live, he knew he would spend his life with her. She'd sewn up his injured side and bandaged his leg with artillery firing not fifty yards away.

Ten years had passed, but there was still no one he'd rather have at his side in a crisis. He could count on Mary to keep her head no matter what befell them.

"I'm glad we left the boys at home," shouted Mary over the noise.

Thurio nodded, saving his breath, relieved that the boys were two hundred miles north in Tuscany. He and Mary had missed them horribly, but now he was glad they had left them with his sister before coming to help Mother convalesce. Antonio and Sebastian were four and two. With Mother injured and Mary soon to have another child, they had decided the boys would only add to the difficulty. Thank God for small blessings.

"How much time do we have?" asked Mary as they ducked between carriages. He barely heard her over the street noise.

The maestro shook his head. "I've no way to know. The wind is against them. That, at least, is in our favor."

Mary gasped and her steps faltered. A dart of fear lodged in Thurio's chest. "What is it, my dear!"

She regained her pace and smiled, wrapping her hands around her stomach. "Our little one is complaining about all the commotion."

Thurio returned her smile but hurried his pace with his heart racing. Everything depended on reaching the ship before it departed.

He jogged the last few blocks with Mary panting as she struggled to keep pace beside him and his mother groaning as she bounced in his arms.

They turned a corner into the harbor. It was nearly deserted of ships, though groups of men fought over a few remaining rowboats. Three ships floated in the bay, their crews working feverishly. Only their ship, the *Anglia*, remained at the wharf. Her sails billowed, and she pulled at the ropes a crewman on the pier was trying to cast off. A handful of townsfolk grabbed at the crewman, begging for passage.

Thurio's heart froze.

"Oh, dear Lord, they're leaving," gasped Mary. She broke into a labored run with Thurio at her side.

The last crewman kicked one of the townsfolk into the water as he climbed up the ship's side. The ship began to move as their footsteps echoed hollowly on the dock.

"Wait," yelled Thurio.

"Come on then!" yelled the captain, waving them on. A dozen weathered, crewmen's faces crowded at the side and tar-stained hands extended over the rail.

The *Anglia* slid forward along the pier. Thurio reached the side, passing desperate townsfolk, and thrust Mother's slight form upward. Sturdy hands caught hold and hoisted her up. She cried in pain as she disappeared over the side. Thurio and Mary hurried along the dock as the ship gained speed.

"Up you go," he said to Mary as he grabbed her hips and lifted her up toward the waiting hands. She raised her arms and curled her legs to protect her stomach. In a moment, she too disappeared aboard.

Thurio reached the end of the planking and leapt for the outstretched palms.

Thurio stooped as he carried Mother into a low, dark cabin and placed her gently on the cot. She stifled a cry of pain. Mary, followed, carrying a glowing lantern, and trailed by three other women. The other women bunched in the doorway, not fitting in the tight space. Mary hung the lantern from a hook and shadows swung across the bare wood walls. The occupants swayed with the ship, and already Thurio felt sick to his stomach. Mary exuded calm among the flustered ladies with pinched faces and wringing hands.

"You should lie down as well," said one of the women to Mary. "It must be well past time for your confinement. The baby could come any moment."

The others nodded their heads and murmured agreement.

"Now don't fuss, ladies," said Mary, wiping her forehead with the heel of her hand and leaning against the wall to brace against the rocking. "I found the whole escapade rather invigorating. And the child will let me know when it's time."

She said to Mother, "I'll get you some water and see if they have a doctor. He might have something for the pain."

"Thank you, dear," she replied.

Mary turned to go but Thurio took her hand and brought it to his lips. She smiled and stroked his cheek before hurrying out with the other ladies following.

Thurio fought down a wave of seasickness. He sat beside Mother and smoothed back her disheveled grey hair. The last half hour had etched the lines in her face deeper.

"Are we safe now?" she asked wearily.

"I hope so," he said, taking her hand.

Tears welled in the corners of her eyes, but she blinked them away. "I couldn't bear to lose you or Mary to those dirty pirates as well."

"You won't. Not if I can help it."

The last time the corsairs attacked he'd been fifteen. He and his family had lived in a small village to the north of Salerno. He had wanted to fight, but his father ordered him to lead his mother and two sisters to safety in the hills. His father and two older brothers had gone to the battle. Only one brother returned.

Thurio had watched from their hiding place above town as the corsairs cut down anyone who opposed them. Then they rounded up everyone they could catch. The pirates weren't after treasure, though they took what they could find. They wanted able bodies—men, women, and children that they could sell. Friends and neighbors were snatched, chained, and carted off—over a thousand of them. Those too old or infirm to sell, the pirates herded into the church. Then they set it on fire.

Thurio shivered remembering the screams, even from a half mile away. That day he took up the sword. Never again would he feel helpless to defend the people he cared about. That day he set upon the road that eventually made him a maestro.

Mary returned, breaking his reverie. "The doctor will be here soon."

He rose, taking a water pitcher and goblet from her. Together they propped Mother up so she could have a drink. She lay back, sighing, and fingering a rosary.

Mary and Thurio sat side by side on the edge of the cot. Mary leaned into him, resting her forehead against his neck. He wrapped his arm around her. She felt warm and soft against him. Mary took his free hand and laid it on the bulk of her belly. He looked at her sharply as he felt the writhe and thump under his hand.

"Good gracious, he's trying to kick his way out," said Thurio.

Mary smiled. "She. I hope it's a girl. There are enough men about the house already."

Thurio chuckled. "With kicks like these? It must be a boy, and a sturdy one at that." He kissed her on the forehead as she laughed with him.

"What shall we call him?" she said, snuggling into his side.

"Well," said Thurio, "considering how hard he's fighting to get loose; his name should be *free*. How about, Francesco."

"A good name," said Mother softly.

"And to think—"

A loud rumbling overhead interrupted Mary.

Thurio's body tensed, and he felt Mary do the same. *Are they rolling out the cannons?* He rose quickly. "I'll see what's happening."

When Thurio climbed awkwardly onto the rolling deck, he squinted into the bright sun. The wind filled the cream-colored sails and thrummed through the rigging. The coast slid past a half mile off their left side. They neared the point just past San Marco, where a flock of gulls circled overhead.

Two-dozen reeling townsfolk stared anxiously over the right-hand rail, getting in the way of the crewmen working the sails. The landsmen looked like merchants and bankers and their families—friends and business associates of the captain he assumed. A quick glance at their frightened faces and the way they held themselves and he summed up their usefulness in a fight—next to none. He hoped he was wrong.

Thurio spotted Captain Sabatini at the starboard rail with a spyglass to his eye and headed toward him. Thurio leaned against the rail for balance, one hand shielding his eyes from the sun, the other rubbing the hilt of the sword at his side. A ship crested the horizon two or three miles behind them, headed directly for them. It had three triangular sails and even without the spyglass Thurio could make out the red flag with a crescent moon and skull at the main mast. The flag of the Barbary Corsairs.

"Pirates," said Thurio.

Captain Sabatini closed his spyglass with a snap and turned to the Thurio. The swarthy captain had a jaw too big for his face and eyebrows that bunched into a line. His disheveled clothes suggested he'd been caught napping by news of the corsairs.

"The pirate fleet's advance scout most likely," said the captain. "She's fast, that's for sure. Faster than us by a long shot."

Thurio turned to gaze ahead. Five distant ships fled, as they did, south along the coast. A few fishing villages dotted the shore, but none had fortifications or defensible positions that he knew of. It looked to be a fight, and while a part of him craved vengeance for his father and brother, a larger part feared for his loved ones in the cabin below. He gripped his sword hilt tighter.

"I'm glad we have your sword on our side," said the captain.

"I'm only sorry that waiting for me put you in a position to need my sword," said the maestro. "You're a good friend."

The captain waved away his words. "I didn't do it for you, old friend, but for that pretty little wife of yours. With her being in a delicate condition and all, I hated to think what those beasts might do to her."

A shiver twanged up Thurio's spine and the captain put a hand on his shoulder. "It'll be two, perhaps three hours before they catch us. Go. Spend some time with your family."

When Thurio returned to the cabin, Mother slept, snoring lightly. Mary sat on the bed at Mother's head, her back against the ship's timbers and her arms draped over her belly. Lantern light turned her skin to gold and her hair bronze. She reached out to him and Thurio took her hand, perching on the cot in front of her.

"The doctor gave her a sleep draught," said Mary, tilting her head toward Mother.

"And how is Francesco?" said Thurio, putting a hand on her stomach. "Has he settled down?"

She nodded, circling her palms on the sides of her tummy. "The ship is rocking him to sleep. What did you find out?"

Thurio ran a hand through his jet-black hair. "There's a corsair chasing us."

"Only one?"

"One is plenty," he said.

"Yes, but better than two, or ten. And they want us alive. They don't want to kill their merchandise."

Thurio's love for her welled up, filling his chest to bursting. She was the only woman he'd ever met who wouldn't be reduced to a quaking mass by news of a pirate battle. Only she could find the bright side of a pirate attack.

He followed her train of thought. "So, they won't use grapeshot to wipe us out," he said. "They'll disable the ship and board. That means close fighting."

She nodded. "And there is no one in the world better at hand-to-hand combat than you, my love."

He ran his hand down her cheek and rested it against her warm neck. "Still, if they disable the ship, we'll drift, helpless. The rest of the fleet could seize us when they caught up. And we'll likely be outnumbered three or four to one considering the way pirates pack their ships with men."

"What if they thought we were surrendering?" said Mary.

"They'd have no cause to disable the ship. They would want to take it as a prize," he said, musing.

"Once they came in close…"

"We could scour their decks with grapeshot," he finished.

Grapeshot, a canvas bag of tightly packed musket balls shot from a cannon, was devastatingly effective against a mass of men. He'd seen it used more than once, thankfully, not toward him. The shot fanned out clearing swaths of bodies at a time.

Mary nodded, as he continued. "We might reduce their numbers by half and double our odds."

His spirits spiked and he leaned forward kissing her on the lips. "I'll talk to the captain. I knew I married you for a reason. You are brilliant, my little Paprika."

She grinned at him. "Of course I am. I married you."

———————⊦———————

Three long, tense hours later, when the corsairs pulled nearly parallel with them, close enough to send a cannonball whizzing past their bow as a warning shot, the captain called, "Heave to!"

The helmsman put the wheel over and the sails fluttered, then fell slack. The *Anglia* slowed, wallowing on the waves. At a word from the captain, a white flag jerked up the mast and flashed against the blue sky. A cheer from the pirate ship reached the *Anglia.*

But behind closed gun ports, the gun crews crouched beside their cannons—cannons primed and loaded with grapeshot. Thurio and the townsmen knelt with muskets ready behind the two inverted longboats stacked between the masts.

Thurio steadied his nerves. He'd been in battles before, too many, but never one where the ground swayed beneath him, or where he had so much to lose if he failed. He forced the thoughts of Mary, Mother, and his unborn child out of his mind. He concentrated on the sway of the deck, judging how it would affect his aim and footing. The pirates with their sea-legs had a clear advantage over a landsman, but he had the best sword arm in Europe, and he had motivation. The pirates would only get to his wife and child over his corpse.

He waited for the captain's signal, fighting the urge to peek at the closing ship. The pirates should pull into the sights of the cannons at any moment. He glanced at the townsmen, sweating, faces taught with fear, knuckles white on the barrels of their muskets, and hoped their nerve held.

"Open fire!" bellowed the captain.

The six right gun ports *thunked* open as Thurio rose. The corsair ship had drawn even with them thirty yards off. Her sails were taut, and foam churned from her bow. At least a hundred corsairs crowded the rail.

Their brightly colored coats and turbans might have looked festive under different circumstances. They waved curved scimitars and muskets, yelling for blood.

Thurio propped the musket he'd been handed on the longboat in front of him and took aim at a man in a blood-red turban, waiting for the rise of the next wave. As he pulled the trigger, the six cannons erupted. Smoke smothered the deck and Thurio ducked down to reload his musket with sure movements. Screams drifted across the water. The townsmen coughed and fumbled, trying to reload their muskets in a panic.

"Bring us to the wind!" yelled the captain. The ship turned, sails swelling. She began to move.

Thurio rose to fire again but could see nothing through the smoke. He couldn't even tell where the corsair was. Then red flashed through the smoke and pirate cannons roared. He aimed just above a flash of red where the gun crew should be and fired.

The *Anglia* jerked and creaked as a barrage of chainshot—two cannonballs with a chain between—ripped through the rigging, some hitting masts and yardarms. The corsairs were trying to disable the ship by taking out their rigging. Wood splinters, severed ropes, and scraps of sail showered the deck. Musket balls from the corsair ship thudded into the wooden boats in front of Thurio. Three crewmen cried out and fell to the deck.

Through thinning smoke Thurio saw that the faster corsair had passed in front of the *Anglia* and tacked. She headed toward them on their left side.

Shouting to the townsmen to follow, Thurio climbed over the longboats to keep them between him and the pirates. He reloaded and awaited their approach. The first barrage of grapeshot had been effective. It looked as though at least a quarter of the pirates had fallen and fans of bright red blood covered what he could see of the pirate deck. But they had only twenty crewmen ready to fight aboard the *Anglia* as well as twenty frightened townsmen. The odds were still bad.

"Hard to starboard!" the captain shouted. "Larboard guns! Give her another broadside!"

The cannons thundered and billowed smoke.

Musket balls peppered the *Anglia*, one ricocheting off the longboat inches from Thurio's face. He flinched away, and then saw her.

Mary knelt over the spasming body of a crewman tying a tourniquet around his ravaged leg. She waved to another crewman yelling, "Take him to the doctor!"

As the corsair came abreast, now only ten yards off, Thurio bolted for Mary. He threw himself to the deck next to her, bringing her down with him and shielding her with his body. The corsair's cannons bellowed. The longboats and ship's rail exploded in splinters that rained down on them. One of the *Anglia's* cannons flew backwards, crushing men beneath it. Grappling hooks snaked out from the pirate ship.

"We must get you below," yelled Thurio.

"Please, Thurio, I can help."

He shook his head. "Not today, my love."

He helped her rise and wrapped his arm around her, hurrying for the companionway stairs. Once they descended to the landing she turned to him. "The women and children are in the great cabin. I'll stay here and defend the door."

He noticed that she wore a sword at her side. Where she had got it, he had no clue.

"No!" he said. "No heroics. You're in no condition."

He had taught her to fence, so he knew her skill. At first, teaching her had been just for fun. When they first got together, she had wanted to be included in that part of his life, so he'd agreed. They kept it secret since most people would have found it scandalous. Somehow, that made it even more fun. Their lessons together had been sensual as he corrected her form and her movements. Though, over time, he'd realized that she had talent, she was lightning quick, with amazing point control. But that was different; a game, a diversion, not life and death, and she hadn't been eight months pregnant.

He tried to usher her toward the great cabin, but she held her ground and faced him.

"I'd rather die fighting than have our child born in slavery," she said. She sounded calm, determined, not panicked like anyone else would have been, and he loved her even more.

She held his eyes. "We both know, if the pirates get this far, those are the only choices."

Ice spread outward from his belly. He wanted to argue, but what could he say? There was no safe place for her to go, nowhere to hide aboard ship where the pirates couldn't find her. Why had he brought them here?

Mary put both hands to his tense jaws, her face hard. "Don't let them get this far."

He nodded once, slowly, with the ice in his stomach turning to steel. He turned and headed up the companionway.

As he emerged on deck, the ship shuddered. A section of wooden hull and the companionway stairs behind him disintegrated into splinters as a cannonball flew through the ship.

Pain seared along Thurio's right side, and he staggered. "Mary!" he yelled as he looked down through the gaping hole that had been the stairs. She had been knocked to the deck. He jumped down past the wreckage and ran to her.

She sat up as Thurio knelt beside her. Small spots of blood appeared on her dusty green dress where slivers of oak had peppered her.

"Are you hurt badly?" said Thurio, scanning her wounds.

She reached up toward her neck.

Then he saw it.

Thurio's breath stopped. The world spiraled and warped around him. A five-inch, ragged splinter protruded from the side of Mary's neck.

"Oh God," he whispered.

Mary's fingers found the intruder, and before Thurio could think or move to stop her, she pulled it free.

Blood had spattered everywhere by the time Thurio set Mary down on the cot next to Mother. Mother held her hand to the wound, blood welling between her fingers, as Thurio sprinted to find the doctor.

He ran blindly, yelling and searching in a surreal daze in which seconds lasted a lifetime and minutes flew by too fast. Finally, he found the doctor in the hold and returned with him in tow.

Thurio knelt at Mary's head as the doctor examined her wound. Her breathing was shallow, but her green eyes locked on Thurio's.

"The baby," she whispered.

She put a weak hand to her stomach and Thurio could see her belly moving through the fabric of her dress.

"Doctor, please," said Thurio, his voice like glass in his throat. "Do something."

"The damage to the vein is too great," said the doctor. "I'm sorry. I can't stop the bleeding."

Thurio clutched the man's bicep and squeezed, willing him to save her. "You must! You have to."

The doctor grabbed Thurio's wrist. He was clearly hurting the doctor, but he didn't care.

"We must take the baby now if it is to survive," the doctor said.

"Take? Oh, God, no." He trembled, letting go of the man's arm.

"I'm sorry, Maestro, but your wife will be dead in minutes and your child will die three minutes later. We cannot save your wife, but your child needn't die."

"Thurio," whispered Mary.

He knelt beside her and took her hand. It felt cold so he tried to knead the warmth back into it.

"Save Francesco," she said to the doctor. Her eyelids fluttered closed, then opened again.

Thurio held her cold hand to his tearstained cheek. "No!"

"Yes, son," said Mother putting a hand on his back. "You must let her go."

Mary sighed and closed her eyes. Her breathing stopped.

Thurio stood. Mary lay still, but the writhing in her belly grew more intense. Francesco fought for life. The doctor stood ready with a scalpel in hand to free him.

Thurio nodded, once.

The doctor went to work. Thurio turned toward the cabin door, drawing his sword.

When Thurio climbed the shattered stairs and arrived on deck, it heaved with fighting men. Fury like he had never known propelled him forward. It filled him so completely that he felt himself on fire, like a god of flame. His sword was Wrath, it sang and hissed against other blades and whispered as it found its targets.

On and on he went for what seemed like forever, slashing and stabbing, watching bodies drop. Once a corsair's scimitar raked down his face filling one eye with blood. It didn't matter, and he didn't feel it. Death does not feel pain.

Eventually, there were no bastards left to slay.

Thurio stood, sides heaving, blood dripping onto the deck. His rage melted, slipping away like a dream upon awakening. In its place flooded despair and pain. *My brave girl. Mary.*

Through the groans of injured and dying men, he heard a baby's wail, high and plaintive. Though his mind felt disconnected, his body moved toward the sound, down the ruined stairs to the closed cabin door.

He couldn't go in. He leaned his head against the door frame as shudders and sobs wracked him.

The door opened. Mother stood with a red-pink squalling child wrapped in a cloth in her arms.

He wiped the blood from his eyes. With a stuttering breath, Thurio took the child, staring at the tiny perfect fingers and the little mewling mouth. He swallowed hard. "Is he going to be all right?"

Mother wiped her eyes. "Francesca is just fine."

He looked up at her. "A girl?"

She nodded.

Thurio leaned back against the doorframe and stared up at the beams, letting the tears flow. "My brave little girl," he said.

FRANCESCA'S FIRST BLADE

Tuscany
June 8th, 1707

With a flurry of anticipation, Francesca bounced down the dark oak stairs to breakfast. Today was her birthday. Today she was seven years old—a big girl. Today was going to be the best day ever, the day that Papa would start her training. He would give her a beautiful, shining blade engraved with her name and the DiCesare coat of arms, like he had for her older brothers Sebastian and Antonio.

Today, with her new blade and her training, she would become a true DiCesare. *Papa said that through all of Europe, the name DiCesare is synn… synom…* She couldn't remember the word. *The name DiCesare means 'skilled with a sword.' I have to be good at fencing.* Sebastian and Antonio were well on their way, and she would be soon too.

She tried not to think about the fact that her brothers had gotten their swords and their training on their sixth birthdays. *It's because I'm a girl,* she told herself. *I was too small last year; I needed another year to grow. But now I'm big.* A worry wormed into her thoughts, but she melted it away with her excitement.

Breathless, she ran into the family dining room, then bit her lip in disappointment. Only Nana had arrived. A small fire crackled merrily in the marble fireplace, glowed off the dark wood paneling, and lit up the tapestries. Nana, stooped and tiny, stood near the fire leaning on her cane. Francesca's oldest brother, Antonio, now twelve, already stood taller than Nana. She opened her arms and Francesca rushed into them.

"There's my sweet girl. Happy birthday." Nana gave Francesca a warm hug. She cupped Francesca's face in her gnarled hands and nodded to a bundle wrapped in sackcloth on the table. "Something to go with your beautiful green eyes."

Francesca unwrapped a lovely, emerald, velvet dress embroidered with silver butterflies. She held it up against herself and swished around the room. "Oh, Nana! It's wonderful. When did you have time to do this?" She knew how much Nana's hands hurt her.

"Oh, a little here, a little there." She smiled.

Francesca heard footsteps in the hall and turned quickly toward the door, but only Antonio and Sebi appeared, already dressed for class in their white fencing jackets. They headed straight for the sideboard to spoon eggs from a silver ewer onto plates as they wished her a happy birthday. Antonio tousled her hair as he passed, and she tried to smooth it back into place. His grey eyes matched Papa's, though without Papa's intensity. Sebi, two years older than Francesca, had green eyes like her, and like the portrait of their mother above the mantle—though Sebi's always seemed mocking. Then Papa's footsteps sounded in the hall and her heart thumped.

Papa entered with his hands behind his back. "There's my brave girl, seven years old and nearly grown." He strode toward her.

His smile didn't reach his grey eyes. He always seemed a little sad on her birthday since it also marked the day her mother died. He bent and kissed her on the top of her head. "Now, for your special gift. I had it made just for you." Francesca's breath caught and her heart pounded as, with a flourish, he presented her gift.

A china doll.

Disappointment crashed down, knocking the breath from her. Her chest caved in.

Papa patted her on the head as he turned toward the eggs on the sideboard.

The doll was beautiful, with auburn hair and green eyes like her, and a dress to match the one Nana had just given her, but she hated it with all her heart.

She dropped it and burst into tears as she ran from the room. With bleary eyes she bolted up a flight of stairs, slammed her door, and threw herself on her peach bedspread. She sobbed into her pillow, crushing it to her face. She had been so sure.

Last year, when she had hoped for her sword and training, Papa had given her a silver locket, engraved with the DiCesare coat of arms, containing an auburn curl of her mother's hair. Francesca loved the gift but couldn't stop her disappointment. Nana had once mentioned that Papa had taught Momma to fence, so she thought the locket meant he would teach her too, eventually. A hundred times last year she had asked Papa if she could start her training. Papa would shake his head and say "No, my Cesca," then send her off to Nana or her governess.

Today was supposed to be different. Surely, she must be big enough now. With no other girls at the salle except servants, she had no way to judge, but she was a DiCesare, surely her lessons must start soon. All the DiCesares fenced, except for Nana, of course, with her gnarled hands and bad hip. Today *had to* be her day.

Papa's footsteps echoed in the hall, and he knocked at her door. "Cesca?"

She didn't answer, but he came and sat down, setting the doll next to her. As she turned her face to the wall she said, "Another whole year?"

He sighed heavily. "I know what you were hoping for," he said. "I'm truly sorry, dear heart, but I can't give you what you want. I won't. Girls don't fence." His voice sounded weary as he rubbed the scar that ran down his forehead and cheek, as he often did when upset.

"Ever?"

"Ever."

She felt a rip, as though half of her had been torn away. *How can I be a DiCesare if I don't fence? And if I'm not a DiCesare, what am I? Nothing. Nobody.* "But. I'm big enough now. And Nana said that even Mamma—"

"I made a mistake. If she hadn't wanted to... If she'd been with the other women... I won't make that mistake again. No."

Francesca curled into the hole in her stomach and gulped air between sobs. He put a warm hand on her back. "I've seen too much in this world, Francesca. Men are brutish, hard. Women and girls are meant for higher things. Like your mother, you are the best of us. You have a beautiful life

17

ahead of you, Cesca. But it cannot include the sword."

He turned her gently to look at him. "It breaks my heart to deny you, but I must. So you must stop asking. I forbid you to ask me again." He kissed her cheek, then rose, and left her with the doll and her tears.

Francesca's disappointment grew hot and transformed into anger. With a shrill scream she threw her pillow as hard as she could at the door Papa had just closed behind him. It made an unsatisfying *poof*. She grabbed her green-eyed doll by one leg, flinging it at the door. It made a much more satisfying *crunch* as the ceramic head caved in. *I am good enough!* She thought, slashing at her tears. *It's not fair! It's not my fault I'm a girl!*

As she looked for something else to smash, she heard Papa and the students outside.

She went to the window. The tan stone villa that made up Salle DiCesare formed a U around the cobblestone courtyard. On the right, a canvas awning striped in orange shaded benches and fencing gear. Beyond the courtyard stood the iron gate and beyond that, the stables, and the rolling green hills.

Class began in the courtyard two stories below. Young men and boys in their white fencing jackets lined up on the left side of the courtyard. Papa called them to attention as he strode to the center of the yard. Francesca wanted to pound on the wavy glass until it crashed down on them. How could he look so calm when he had just destroyed her whole world? What made those boys so much better than her?

The students took their *en garde* positions, knees bent, back straight, right shoulder and knee forward and blades ready. She watched through tears as papa walked among them correcting their form.

A soft rapping came at her door. Nana's knock.

Francesca reluctantly opened the door. Her new birthday dress draped over one of Nana's arms. Nana tilted her head to the side and said, "That won't do. Those red eyes are going to clash with your new dress."

"Don't tease, Nana. Not today." Francesca sat back down on her bed dropping her head and wiping at tears.

Nana pushed the remains of the doll aside with her foot, picked the pillow off the terracotta floor and tossed it next to Francesca. She laid the dress down on the end of the bed. "I'm sorry, dear. But there's no use crying over what can't be helped. If there were, the world would be drowning in tears."

Francesca hunched her shoulders. She could feel Nana's soft, dove grey eyes sizing her up.

Nana said "Come, dear. Why don't you help your old grandmother collect some flowers for the dinner table tonight? The garden always cheers you up."

Francesca glowered toward the window but nodded.

"Good. Then you can help me back down the stairs, it was a bear to get up here with this old hip."

———⊥———

After Francesca helped Nana down the stairs, through the kitchen to collect a basket and a knife, and out into the garden, they found Nana a seat on a bench facing the roses. Gravel paths radiated out from the circular bed of roses at the center of the garden. Usually, Francesca loved to run up and down the paths, delighting in the bright colors of the flowers against the green leaves, as the smells of lavender and rosemary blew on the breeze. But today she didn't feel like it.

The early morning's sun had given way to low, gathering clouds and a wet wind, promising rain later.

"Bring me five of those bright red roses," said Nana. "And mind you cut the stems long."

As Francesca walked glumly toward the roses, she thought about their visit last spring to Sr. Alba's pig farm. She and her brothers had watched the squirming, squealing, pink piglets and Sebi had pointed out a tiny runt half the size of the others. When it tried to squeeze in to get a drink of milk, its mother ignored it and its brothers and sisters kicked and bit it until it crawled away into a corner of the pen, outcast. Sr. Alba told them the runt was too weak and would die within a few days. That's what she felt like, too weak and useless to be a DiCesare. Why had she even been born?

As she returned, flowers in hand, she saw Nana rubbing her hip, her forehead scrunched in pain. "Bad today?" she asked.

Nana nodded. "These weather changes have played havoc with it since it broke."

"You never told me how you broke it?"

Nana gave a chuckle, "Doing something I wasn't supposed to."

Francesca's eyes widened. "What were you doing?"

Nana leaned closer to her and dropped her voice, though no one could hear. "Jumping my horse Carrots over a hedge."

Francesca stared at Nana, who laughed. "Don't look at me like that. And close your mouth, its unladylike. I'll have you know I was quite a rider back in my day."

"Really?" She couldn't imagine Nana on the back of a horse, much less jumping a hedge.

"Carrots was a natural jumper and I loved it as much as she. When I was young, my parents forbade me. As did your grandfather when we first married—as if I would listen. I gave it up after I had the children, and while they were young. They needed me. But after they'd grown, I started again. Your grandfather used to say it was unladylike, but I think that was part of the fun. Now, go cut three of the pink dahlias."

Francesca wandered to the dahlias trying to imagine Nana sneaking away to jump her horse. As she added the new flowers to Nana's basket she asked, "Do you regret it?"

Nana waved her words away. "No. I'm sorry I fell, but Carrots and I jumped for many years, and it brought us both a great deal of pleasure. Seven of the white roses, the ones that smell especially good, if you please."

When Francesca returned, Nana held the roses to her face and inhaled the sweet scent. "You know, my dear, there are two things people can regret in life. Doing something, and not doing something. Not doing something leaves you the poorer. At least if you regret something you've done, you have had the experience." She looked at Francesca and lowered her eyebrows. "Within reason, of course. As long as no one gets hurt."

Francesca nodded. Nana seemed to be trying to tell her something, but she didn't know what.

"How about some rosemary for the scent," said Nana.

Francesca hurried off toward the bed of rosemary bushes. On the way, she passed beneath the old oak and noticed a branch on the ground about the length and width of a practice foil. She picked it up, but it only made her sadder. She felt like she had a big hole inside of her ribs. She went back with the rosemary, swishing the stick against the foliage along the path. "Nana?" she said as she added the rosemary to the basket, "why won't Papa teach me to fence?"

"What did he say?"

"He said boys are bad and girls are better, but it doesn't seem that way. It feels like he means that I'm not good enough. I never will be. And if girls are better, why do we have to have so many rules? It's not fair."

"Well, my dear, in my experience, the world is very seldom fair. Especially to women. But that doesn't make them not good enough."

"You said he taught mamma."

"Hmm, yes, I probably shouldn't have told you that. It's complicated. I don't know exactly why he won't teach you, but the decision is his, so you'll need to honor that."

"So, I'll never get to learn." She poked the stick into the gravel at their feet.

"Come, help me up. We'll take these inside before the rain comes. We can collect some more greens on the way." Nana took Francesca's arm and leaned on her. Francesca carried the basket and stick in the other hand.

Nana said offhandedly, "You know, teaching and learning are two different things. No one taught Carrots and me how to jump."

Papa usually insisted they all eat together, but he never showed up when the family gathered for lunch. Antonio said he had ridden into Casina shortly after fencing class. Francesca was glad he'd left. She flipped back and forth between two emotions. Half the time she still felt angry with him, and wondered if he didn't want to face her after their breakfast scene. But the rest of the time she felt ashamed of being a girl and not being worth teaching. That part made her want to cry again.

She spent the afternoon in history and piano classes and polishing the silver with her governess, Senora Álvarez, and then helping Nana arrange the flowers they had picked.

Wearing her new green dress, she entered the dining room for her birthday dinner. Sebi and Antonio looked up as she entered, and Sebi laughed. "You look like a frog." He stuck his tongue out, like a frog catching a fly.

Antonio swatted him with the back of his hand. "Don't be a pig. You look nice, Francesca."

"You're the bug." She stuck out her tongue at Sebi. "I'll eat you up." But she responded from habit, and she felt even more worthless.

Papa entered pushing Nana in her rolling chair. "Marvelous!" said Papa, "we're all here." He seemed excited and happy, but it seemed wrong somehow, and Francesca couldn't meet his eyes all dinner. She felt ashamed of being a no-good runt. She didn't even look at him when he said, "Cesca, there will be a surprise for you in the morning. For now, let's just celebrate our brave girl."

I hope it's not another doll, thought Francesca, hiding a grimace as the servants brought in their dinner.

———+——

Papa woke her early. Bleary-eyed, she followed him down the stairs, out the double doors of the villa. The sun, barely up, painted the courtyard peach. She yawned as they passed through the wrought iron gate of the salle toward the stables where the sun glowed orange off the terracotta tile roof and yellow off the tan stones of the walls. She gave Papa a confused look as he opened the corral gate behind the stable and ushered her in.

Cassio, the head groom held the end of a rope around the neck of a beautiful black foal. It had long, delicate legs and an elegantly arched neck. Francesca gasped as Cassio gestured toward her with the rope.

"For me?" she asked.

"You're the birthday girl," Papa said, grinning.

Francesca's heart melted and expanded at the same time. She wanted to run to the colt and throw her arms around it, but she approached cautiously, not wanting to spook it.

"Don't be shy," said Cassio, "he's not."

She held out her hand as she neared, and the foal sniffed and nibbled at her fingers with rubbery lips. He let her stroke his head, then she wrapped her arms around his neck and hugged him. The colt pressed into her arms and rubbed his jowls against her. Francesca thought her heart might explode from so much love. She blinked away tears. "What's his name?"

"That's up to you," said Papa.

The colt pulled away and Cassio removed the rope letting him run and caper around the corral.

Papa put a hand on her shoulder. "This is a big responsibility, Cesca. He's just weaned, and he'll need a lot of care."

"That's for certain," said Cassio. "At his age, he's growing so fast he'll need twice the food of a horse full grown. And he'll need brushing, training, and socializing."

"Yes! Oh yes! I'll do all of it! Thank you, Papa!" She hugged him, squeezing as tight as she could. She watched the colt running and kicking up his heels. His jet-black coat gleamed in the sunshine, except for one white patch on the back of his front right fetlock. "Look. He has an Achilles heel. That must be where God held him when he dipped him in black ink and made him all shiny."

Papa laughed. "It must be. Is that his name then? Achilles?"

"Of course!"

She spent half the morning with Achilles and Cassio, learning how to brush, feed, and exercise her colt. And they started training him.

As she headed back into the salle to help Sra. Álvarez with the mending, Papa worked in the courtyard, teaching the older students advanced fencing skills, working with a rapier in one hand and a dagger in the other. Despite the happiness of the last few hours, her sorrow and shame crashed back down on her. She knew Papa gave her Achilles to distract her from not being good enough to fence. She also knew it wouldn't work.

When she stopped in her room to clean up, she saw the branch she had found the day before and thought of Nana's words. "No one taught Carrots and me how to jump." She glanced out the window at the students. *Nana taught herself how to jump her horse. Maybe I could teach myself how to fence. Is that what Nana was telling me? If I learn on my own, then, would I still not be good enough? Would that make me a DiCesare? Does it count if no one else knows I'm doing it?*

Those seemed like big questions, and she didn't know the answers. She gnawed on a fingernail as she stared out the window at Papa teaching an advanced move outside.

She turned at a light knock on her open door. Two of the laundry maids curtsied, eyes cast down. One of them gestured toward her bed. "May we, Signorina?"

When Francesca nodded, they hurried to the bed and expertly stripped the sheets to be washed. Francesca started to turn back to the window but stopped to watch them.

Bianca, sixteen, had a lot of muscle from dealing with all the wet linens. She, and her sister Elena who was thinner and fourteen, both had circular faces with round noses and chins, and watery eyes beneath thin, arched eyebrows. Their cheeks flared red as they whispered to each other, glanced at Francesca, and quickly dropped their eyes, just as she'd been doing to Papa all day. She recognized that 'not good enough' gesture. The girls gathered up the sheets and curtsied again as they hurried out.

Francesca followed, stopping in her doorway to watch them go into Sebi's room next door. Leaning against the doorframe, she thought again about her question of yesterday. *If I'm not a DiCesare, what am I?* She was already hemming her brothers' clothes, fixing their ripped fencing jackets, polishing the silver they used, now not meeting their eyes. *Am I a servant as well? Is that all I'll ever be?*

The maids came out of Sebi's room with arms full of sheets. They bobbed a curtsey as they passed her, carefully avoiding her eyes, and hurried toward the servants' stairs.

Tears threatened to well up again. *I'm a servant with pretty dresses and a horse.*

Antonio came around the corner from his room down the hall with a cup and saucer in hand. "Ah, Francesca," he said, walking over to her and handing her the cup and saucer. "Be a good girl and take this down to the kitchen for me." He turned and walked away without waiting for an answer.

Francesca's breath huffed out as a cough. Anger and humiliation warred in her stomach, making her feel sick. Anger won. "No!" she shouted at Antonio's back. She stomped over to him as he turned toward her. She shoved the cup and saucer into his chest, and he wrapped his hands around them. "I'm your sister, not your servant!" She stomped back to her room and turned toward him, hand on the door. His eyes were wide in surprise. "I'm not a runt. I won't be. And you can't make me!" She slammed the door.

I'm a real DiCesare! I'm as good as they are. I'm a fencer! She flourished the branch she had found like a blade. Somehow, just that action made her feel better. Like a person again, someone who counted. She looked out the window, at Papa teaching below. *Someday you'll know I'm a fencer. For now, I'll know.*

Slowly, her anger faded. She regarded the branch. If she was going to do this, she wanted to do it right. The branch weighed almost nothing. *It's too light. I need something heavier, like a real blade.*

She opened the window. A rack of fencing gear stood under the canvas awning to her right. She could just take one, but Papa would notice if one suddenly went missing. What would he do then? She couldn't be sure, but it seemed risky. *How do I get a blade?* She pondered the question as she hurried to see her governess who was probably waiting for her impatiently by now.

A spinning wheel stood in one corner of the bright, sunny sewing room. Francesca and her governess sat on comfy brocade chairs. Sra. Álvarez taught Francesca how to darn some of her brothers' wool socks with holes in the toes. Francesca wanted to refuse, but didn't relish a lecture from her governess, so she gritted her teeth and fixed Sebi's socks. Then they worked on repairing frayed hems and torn seams on some of the fencing jackets. With so many growing boys and young men at the salle, something always needed repair.

As her governess turned to speak with one of the maids, Francesca slipped one of the badly torn jackets deep under her armchair. She'd pick it up later and take it to her room. She didn't know what she would do with it, but it seemed like a fencer should have a fencing jacket and she was going to be a fencer.

As she descended the stairs to dinner that evening, Sebi walked down the steps with her, teasing her as usual. "I hear your new horse is black, just like your soul."

"Yeah? Well, well, your horse is the color of poop. Just like *your* soul."

Sebi laughed and Francesca bristled. Later, as she looked at Sebi across the dinner table, she thought, *maybe I can't just take a blade without getting caught, but Sebi could lose one, and I could find it. Then he'd get in trouble, not me.* She licked her lips, the thought of getting Sebi in trouble seemed extra delicious.

It took Francesca nearly a week to catch Sebi at just the right time. She needed to get his attention while he had a practice blade in his hand. Then she needed to distract him enough that he'd forget he held it. She decided her best bet was right after fencing class when she would be coming back from working with Achilles anyway.

The first day she had stood in the cobbled courtyard, just inside the main gate as the students finished their lessons. Moments after Papa called, "Dismissed" she called "Sebi!" He looked at her, rolled his eyes, and turned away to talk to one of the other students as they wandered toward the weapons rack. She curled her hands into fists, awash with anger and shame.

The next day, when she called him, he walked to the fencing rack and put his blade away before coming over to her.

"What is it?" he demanded.

She stammered. "I, well, I…" she hadn't thought of what to say if he didn't have his practice blade. She lied. "Sr. Gallo wants to talk to you about your history lesson." Sr. Gallo had said no such thing, but everyone knew Sebi hated history and never did his schoolwork. So, there was at least a chance she spoke the truth. He grumbled as he turned toward the salle.

Two days later, she called him again. This time he walked over with his blade and her hopes rose. "What do you want," he asked.

"Well, I was hoping that you could help me with Achilles' training."

"Go talk to Cassio. I'm busy." He walked away before she could think of anything else to say.

Today, when class ended, she called to him, "I bet Achilles is better behaved on a lunge line than Arrow." She felt a little ridiculous. Sebi's horse, Arrow, a two-year-old gelding, was saddle trained, and Achilles was a high-spirited colt, but she knew Sebi couldn't resist a bet.

Sebi scoffed, walking in her direction still carrying his practice blade. "What are you talking about? Are you stupid?"

"Achilles behaved perfectly on the lunge line today. And we all know how Arrow likes to misbehave."

Sebi laughed. "I don't believe you. Achilles is a colt. He won't do more than three circuits on the lunge line before he gets distracted."

"I'll bet you a week's worth of chores that he can do five," said Francesca. She'd lose, but it would be worth a week of chores to get a foil.

"Deal," said Sebi, shaking his head in amusement and turning toward the weapons rack.

Francesca nearly panicked. "Now," she said, "or the bet's off."

"Fine," said Sebi, heading out the gate toward the corral. "You'll have to clean up the school rooms every night for a week, and there are three saddles Papa wants me to polish."

"And what if I win," said Francesca.

"Don't worry. You won't."

When they entered the corral, Achilles kicked and bucked playing with a one-year-old bay with a white blaze on her forehead and a two-year-old dapple. The trio nudged each other as they ran around the pen. "You get the rope," said Francesca to Sebi as she called Achilles to her.

Sebi set his blade on the ground next to the gate and ducked inside the stable. She smiled to herself. Nana liked to say, 'out of sight, out of mind.'

So, with Sebi gone, Francesca scooped up an armful of alfalfa from the feed bin and dropped it on top of the practice foil. She hoped Nana was right.

They slipped the knotted rope over Achilles' head and coaxed him to run in a circle around them as they turned to face him. He cooperated for one and a half circuits before he ran back to Francesca for some ear scratching as she lectured him on behaving.

Sebi crowed with delight at getting out of weeks' worth of work. Then he brought out Arrow, his chocolate brown horse, to show off to Francesca. After that, they played with the colts until one of the kitchen boys called them to lunch.

Foil long forgotten, Sebi headed toward the villa. Francesca lagged behind, saying she needed to ask Cassio a question, then, filled with glee, hid the practice blade in Achilles' stall to pick up later. For the price of a few simple chores, she'd gotten a blade.

The next morning at breakfast, Francesca hid her smile as Sebi got a lecture from Papa about losing his belongings.

Afterwards, as class began outside her bedroom window, she took her *en garde* position with her new fencing foil in hand. She watched them for a moment as Papa called, "Advance. Advance, Retreat, Lunge." Then she fell into *en garde* position and followed his orders, advancing across her room from her window to her door and back again. A thrill of pride ran through her. *I'm doing it! I'm fencing.* She couldn't remember ever being happier. *Today I'm a real DiCesare.*

Papa called a halt and had the students pair off. Francesca laughed. Now she knew what to do with that fencing jacket. She pulled it out of her closet along with a petticoat she'd outgrown and stuffed the petticoat inside of it. It could use some more stuffing, but it was a start. "It's nice to meet you, Signore," she said as she propped it up on her bed. She saluted her new opponent, then skewered it with her blade. *"Touché."*

SIGNORE DAMPIER

Tuscany
September 10th, 1708

Francesca slammed her oak bedroom door and threw herself onto her peach bedspread and punched her pillow. It was happening again. In a few days, Papa would leave. He'd be gone for weeks, taking Antonio and Sebastian with him. Once more, she would have to stay home. *Left behind. Abandoned. I never get to go anywhere! It's not fair!*

Francesca wanted to see the whole world. Everywhere else seemed so much more fascinating than home. But no. She had to stay here with Nana. It wasn't her fault she was only eight, or that she was a girl. *Not that I don't love spending time with Nana, but still...*

This time, Antonio and Sebastian would get to see Salerno, Papa's hometown, and she wouldn't. Antonio would get to spend his thirteenth birthday with their aunts and cousins, and she couldn't. Just last month Papa had taken her brothers to Livorno and not her. Last year they even went to Sienna and Florence without her.

She sat up. "Fine," she said to her empty bedroom. "If they won't take me on *their* adventures, I'll go on my own!" She stuck out her tongue at her bedroom door and her family beyond, who were probably still at dinner.

Papa had looked very patient between bites of his lamb shank when he had explained that he didn't want to take the carriage in case Nana needed it to go to town. That he and Sebi and Antonio would go on horseback, which he preferred to the rattling, dusty carriage. Papa had waved his fork as he said that her horse, Achilles, was too young and high-spirited for such a trip and she was too inexperienced as a rider.

She had argued, of course. Maybe Achilles did love to run a bit wild, and maybe he startled easily, but a trip like this would teach him better. And she and Achilles could ride together forever. She knew it. She wouldn't hold them back. She wouldn't.

Then Papa got that look—the set jaw, thin lips, and narrowed grey eyes. The one that meant that he had made up his mind, and nothing she could say would change it. That's when she had thrown down her napkin, yelled that it wasn't fair, and stormed up the stairs.

But where should I go on my *adventure*, she mused. She couldn't just follow them.

I could go to Florence. Sebi described it as a place full of palaces, important people and art works by great artists. That sounded amazing. Or Sienna. Antonio had talked about the horse race in the main square. That sounded exciting too. *But that would be copying what they already did. I want to do something better. Something they never even dreamed of.*

She paced the terracotta tiles of her bedroom. She stopped at the window looking past the empty cobblestone courtyard, to the hills in the distance beyond the gate. The world lay out there, waiting. Where could she go that would make her brothers' jaws drop in amazement and envy?

As she turned, her glance fell on the bookshelf over her bed. *Of course!* One of the books was called *A New Voyage Around the World*. She'd borrowed it from Sebi, who had borrowed it from Papa. While she didn't understand some of it, she loved the part about an amazing place the author visited— about the strange rats as tall as a man that jumped on big hind feet and carried pouches for their babies, and about the dark-skinned, painted natives. *That must be the most interesting place in all the world. That's it! I'll go to Australia! Sebi and Antonio have never been across the sea! Of course, I'll be gone for weeks. Sebi and Antonio will be so jealous! And Papa will miss me, and he'll be sorry that he didn't bring me along.*

Now that she had figured out where, she needed to figure out how. One thing she knew for certain. Eight-year-old girls never ran away to have adventures, but eight-year-old boys might. As far as she could tell, boys could do just about anything they wanted. *So, I need to be a boy. Well, I can manage that. How hard can it be if Sebi can do it?*

She opened her door and peeked out. The hall and classroom stood empty. She moved quietly past Sebi's room, listening for a moment at his door. Everyone was probably still at dinner. She listened at the top of the stairs, but only heard the normal babble of a school full of students eating in the main hall. She went back to Sebi's room slipping inside.

It took only a few moments in his armoire to find an old pair of breeches he'd outgrown and a white, wide-collar shirt he seldom wore. He'd notice if one of his frock coats went missing, but she borrowed a faded, dark blue vest. She rolled everything up and hurried back to her room. Her riding boots would work, but she'd need to do something about her hair. Long hair would be a dead giveaway.

She snuck down to the sewing room, waited for the scullery maid to finish lighting the fire in the hearth, then went to her governess' sewing box rummaging through until she found the scissors. Signora Alvarez would be cross, but Francesca would bring them back when she returned.

Back in her room, she pulled out her valise, frowning at the embroidered daisies covering it. *No boy would be seen dead carrying that, but there might be something in the storage room.* She snuck past her governess' room, pausing when she heard a rustling inside, but she made it safely. She searched quietly among old toys, linens, and disused coats until she found a brown leather shoulder bag with a wide flap over the top, perfect for an overseas adventure.

Once in her bedroom, she loaded the bag with Sebi's clothes, the scissors, a spare pair of stockings, and a few handfuls of almonds, pistachios, and walnuts tied up in a cloth. Then she added the book about Dampier's voyage so she could read about Australia again.

She was ready. She went to the window and swung it open. She *could* start now, but the sun had set, and a chill breeze blew in sending a shiver down her spine. Moon shadows crept across the road beyond the gate, dark and menacing. She wanted to be brave, but it felt a lot easier when the sun shined.

The chamber maid knocked, coming to help her undress for bed. *In the morning*, she thought. *I'll leave first thing.*

She had trouble falling asleep. Fear and excitement swirled in her stomach, like she'd eaten a dozen live snakes. She stared at the ceiling and thought about Dampier's voyage. He had taken months to reach Australia, but then, he had stopped at many strange places along the way. *If I go straight there, I should be there in a few days. Maybe I should bring a rope as a leash so I can bring*

one of the jumping rats home. Otherwise, Sebi and Antonio might not believe I went at all.
After that, she faded into sleep.

In the morning, Francesca jumped out of bed and hurriedly dressed in her riding habit. It was her only outfit that didn't lace up the back and the jacket was masculine enough to work with Sebi's clothes. She slung the leather bag over her shoulder then paused. She should leave word, so they didn't worry too much. At her desk she scribbled a note:

> Dear Papa,
> I went to Australia. Enjoy Salerno. I'll be back soon.
> Love, Francesca.

That ought to make Sebi and Antonio green with envy.

Only servants stirred as she hurried downstairs and out to the stables. The sky was clear, the air crisp, with a touch of the coming fall stinging her cheeks. Even the hay in the stable smelled fresh and bright. Maybe it was the promise of adventure that made everything so sharp and clear.

In the tack room, she found a length of rope curled on a hook and added it to her bag. Achilles tossed his head in excitement when she slipped into his stall.

Usually, Cassio helped her saddle Achilles, but she didn't see him, so she bridled him and hauled the heavy sidesaddle onto his back on her own. As she led Achilles out and climbed into the saddle, she spotted Cassio beside the stable. She wanted to tell him goodbye and to ask if it was alright to keep a jumpy rat in the stable, but it was safer not to say anything. Cassio waved as she rode off.

Francesca rode downhill through the red-leafed grape vines, dying back for the winter. She needed someplace secluded to transform into a boy and the abandoned barn would be perfect. After that, she would head to Cascina, and the road beyond would take her to Livorno where she could find a ship to Australia.

Achilles' hooves rustled through leaflitter as they left the vineyard and entered the woods. The wind swirled gold and yellow leaves past. Once out into the pasture, the sheep, plump with wool, stared up at her. She soon came to the tumbled down barn, now just three grey stone walls at the edge of the pasture.

Dismounting and leaving Achilles to nibble grass, she took her bag into the barn, looked around carefully, then stripped out of her riding habit and petticoats and pulled on Sebi's breeches and shirt. The shirt hung loose, but not horribly so, and once she put on the vest and her coat, it worked reasonably well. The breeches though, would not stay up. They were way too big. Luckily, she had the rope for her jumpy rat. She used it as a belt, wrapping it around and around her waist.

Then she rummaged in the bag and pulled out the scissors. She paused. This was what Nana called a crossroads moment. One way or the other. She could either go home or go on. She remembered another of Nana's sayings. "Strength and courage, for life is a passage." She grabbed a handful of hair, raised the scissors, and snipped. The handful came loose, and she looked at it for a moment, auburn strands wafting in the breeze. She opened her hand and watched it float away, suddenly foreign, like a sea creature swimming through air. She grabbed handful after handful and cut it away. She wished she had thought of bringing a mirror, but too late now.

As she searched her head for stray hairs, she heard leaves rustling and voices approaching.

Oh, no! I'm not ready! She wanted to practice walking and talking like a boy before anyone saw her. Maybe she could hide.

She rolled up her skirts and petticoats quickly and stuffed them and the scissors into the bag. It took a lot of shoving to get it to close. She meant to hide, but she was kicking the pile of hair behind a rock and pulling her bangs down over her face when Antonio rode from behind some bushes on his chestnut horse, Brutus. Maria, an eleven-year-old girl who was learning to be a dairy maid rode behind him, her arms wrapped around his waist. She swung her feet carelessly and chattered to Antonio.

Antonio, who was nearly thirteen, four and a half years older than Francesca, had dark hair and high cheekbones like papa, and papa's long lanky build. He reigned in Brutus, looking at Francesca with his head tilted to one side.

Maria was a golden-haired girl with warm-colored, creamy skin and bright red cheeks. Her eyes and mouth opened wide in surprise. "What on Ear—" she yelped a little and took her arms from around Antonio, staring at him and rubbing a spot on her wrist.

Antonio took off his tricorn hat with a smile. "Good day, young sir," he said. "It's a pleasure to meet you. I'm Antonio DiCesare, and this is Maria. And who might you be?"

Francesca panicked. At least he didn't recognize her, but she should have come up with a name! *Why didn't I think of that?* Luckily Antonio and Maria were dismounting, and whispering together, which gave her a moment to think. She tried to stand like Sebi did, chest puffed out, leaning casually against the stone wall of the barn, with an arrogant tilt to her head.

Only one name came to mind, the name of the author of the book in her bag. She dropped her voice low. "My name is William Dampier. It's a pleasure to meet you."

Maria stepped forward, as if to say something, but Antonio tugged her backwards stepping in front of her saying. "So, Signore Dampier, what brings you to our land?"

"Oh, well," she said with a small cough at keeping her voice low, "I was just passing through and saw this tumbled down barn and thought it a good place to rest."

"Of course," said Antonio. With another tilt of his head he added, "You look strangely familiar."

"I don't think we've met," she replied, glad that it was Antonio and not Sebi. Sebi would have recognized her right away.

"And where are you headed, if I may ask?"

Francesca looked at her nails and tried to sound unconcerned. "I'm going to Australia, of course. It's the most amazing place in all the world."

Antonio gave a small cough, and Maria gave a huff. Maria began, "That's completely—" Then Antonio turned to her quickly, put an arm around her shoulder and turned them both away. They spoke together quietly, and Francesca tried to hear what they were saying, but only made out Maria's shrill, "won't believe," and "can't be serious."

Francesca was inching closer to listen when Antonio turned back to her with a smile. "What my friend meant to say is 'that is completely amazing.' Neither of us have met a world traveler so young as yourself before."

Maria gave Antonio a glare. "I'm going," she said with another huff. She turned to Francesca. "Safe travels, Signore Whatever." Then she stalked back across the sheep pasture shaking her head.

"Never mind her," said Antonio. "We men know what a pain girls can be."

"Yes, of course," said Francesca, a little vexed. "Such a pain." She wanted to ask what he was doing, riding around with the new dairy maid, especially when he was always saying how annoying girls were, but she didn't think a stranger would mention it.

"Take my little sister, for instance. All she does is ride her horse and complain."

Francesca stuck her chin out, but he continued, turning toward Achilles, grazing nearby. "What a coincidence, my sister has a horse very much like yours. What's his name?"

Her mind went blank. "I, I just call him Horse."

"Hmmm," said Antonio, sitting down on a fallen bit of wall. "So, tell me about this trip, please. It sounds fascinating."

"Australia is just the most interesting place ever. They have big jumping rats and painted people. It's on the other side of the world. Australia is much more interesting than any place my brothers have been."

Antonio smiled. "I'm sure. And how long does it take to get there?"

"Oh, a week sailing at least. Maybe two or three. I'm headed to Cascina now, and then to the port to find a ship."

Antonio looked astonished. "Well, what do you know, I happen to be headed to Cascina as well. Let's ride together, shall we?"

Francesca hesitated. Part of her worried that Antonio would see through her disguise, or she'd say something to give herself away, but a larger part wanted the company. Riding into town alone seemed scary. "Yes, let's."

They gathered their horses and Francesca's bag and mounted. She remembered at the last moment to ride astride like a boy. It felt uncomfortable with her sidesaddle, but she managed, hoping Antonio wouldn't notice the saddle. Turning downhill, they crunched through the dead leaves of the forest toward the main road to Cascina. Neither said anything until they gained the road. Then they rode side by side.

"This trip of yours fascinates me," Antonio told her. "All that travel must be quite an ordeal for a young man such as yourself. What made you decide to go so far away?"

"Oh, no. Traveling isn't an ordeal, it's an adventure! The best adventure. Everything is new and different. I can't imagine anything more exciting than seeing a whole new place that is unlike anything you've seen before." She realized she'd let her voice rise to its normal tone in her excitement, so she cleared her throat and dropped her voice low again. It took on more of a bitter tone than she intended. "I don't want to go somewhere boring, like the rest of my family. I want to go somewhere better. Then they'll see."

"I'm sure they will," murmured Antonio. "Won't they be worried about you?"

She glanced over at him. "No. I don't think they'll miss me. They never pay much attention to me. And anyway, I left a note."

"That's not true." Then he added, "I'm sure they would miss you."

She shrugged. "They won't even be around. My grandmother will miss me, though."

They rode on for a while, winding between hills and woods before Antonio said. "You must be brave to go on such a dangerous trip, what with pirates, and storms, and shipwrecks and such. I know I would be scared."

Francesca felt her shoulders tighten and gripped the reigns harder. She hadn't thought about those things. "I'm not scared," she lied. She focused on the big jumping rats. "It will be amazing."

Antonio shifted in the saddle. "Travel isn't *all* great. I've traveled a bit with my father, and as I'm sure you know, sometimes it is pretty uncomfortable." He went on to tell her about how saddle sore he got riding long distances, and about sometimes not being able to find lodging along the way, once even having to sleep outside on the ground.

Francesca only half listened, thinking about pirates and storms. They fell silent for a while, listening to the clop of the horses' hooves and the twitters of birds. As they were passing a few farms on the outskirts of town, Antonio said, "You must be well-off. I imagine a voyage of that length must be quite expensive, especially if you plan to bring your horse, Horse."

Francesca furrowed her brow. "Is it?" That hadn't occurred to her, though now it seemed obvious. "I mean, well, yes, of course. I... I was..."

"I see," he said as she floundered. "You're planning to work for your passage. I'm sure they can use a strong back, and you look like a stout fellow. They'll have you swabbing decks and hauling ropes in no time."

Francesca nodded, a little stunned. She had been so focused on Australia; she hadn't really thought about getting there. Her excitement waned, but she rallied. It was only a week, and she didn't mind hard work if it meant she could go somewhere special—and make her brothers jealous. "Maybe I can even climb up the mast and be a lookout."

He turned to look at her and his eyes lingered for a while. "You are brave, aren't you."

Francesca smiled, though she felt less brave by the minute.

They had passed the church and graveyard where Francesca's mother was buried and were entering the town center. She had been there often for crowded market days or to go to church on holidays. Today seemed eerily quiet. There were only a few booths set up in the main square and a handful of people wandered past, going about their business.

"Are you thirsty?" Antonio asked. "Can I buy you a drink to wish you *bon voyage?*"

Francesca nodded, realizing how dry and scratchy her throat felt from speaking so low. Antonio led the way to a disreputable looking taverna and dismounted. Francesca pulled back. She'd never been in a drinking establishment like this. Nana and Signora Alvarez would be scandalized to see a good girl in there, then she remembered that she was now a boy, and dismounted from Ach... Horse. She nervously followed Antonio inside.

The dark interior smelled of stale ale and the old straw strewn on the floor. At that early hour, only a few men lounged around the tables, most sitting alone, some eating, all nursing drinks. Francesca wondered if Antonio had been here before, or if he came here often. She didn't think Papa would approve. She realized she didn't know much about what her oldest brother did with his spare time. She didn't know that much about him at all.

Antonio pointed her toward a chair and headed to the bar. Francesca sat nervously, fidgeting and pushing her chopped hair out of her eyes, scanning the men in the room. She wasn't sure what she thought they might do, fight, murder each other, murder her? Most just stared at their drinks.

Antonio spoke with the man behind the bar for quite a long time. Occasionally they would both stop to look over at her. She wondered what they were talking about. Finally, the big man laughed, tousled Antonio's hair and slid two tankards across the bar. Antonio took a few coins from his pocket for the man, then came toward Francesca with the drinks.

Antonio slid a tankard across to her and took a sip of his own as he sat down. She thanked him and took a taste, wrinkling her nose. Beer wasn't new to her; they sometimes had a little with dinner. But this was darker and tasted much stronger than what she'd had before. Still, she felt thirsty, and it was wet. She took a couple gulps.

Antonio leaned back in his chair, smiling. "The barkeep, Fredrico, used to be a sailor. I asked if he'd come over and tell us about his adventures. I thought you might like to hear."

Francesca nodded enthusiastically.

Fredrico wandered over to their table wiping his hands on a rag. He was a big man, balding, and plump around the middle, but with massive forearms and a friendly smile. He put one foot up on a chair and leaned his elbow on his knee. "Greetings, lad. Antonio tells me you're thinking of going to sea."

"Yes, sir," said Francesca, trying to match the man's bass voice. "I want to go to Australia."

The big man's face went dark, and he gave a shiver. "Oh, no lad. You don't want to go there. Even the bravest seamen don't want to go there. Why, that's the reason I gave up the sea and work here, well inland." He gave another shudder and made a face. "Australia."

A chill lodged in Francesca's stomach, and she took another gulp to warm it. "Why? What happened?"

Fredrico took a seat and absently wiped the table with the rag. "I'll tell ya. I was crewing on a ship called the *Augustina*. We were off Cape Doubtfire with clear skies, a steady wind abaft our beam, running at ten knots when we, quite literally, ran into a horrible beast."

Francesca took another sip. Her head felt a little fuzzy and fear knotted in her stomach, but she couldn't look away from the storyteller.

"First there came this thump and shudder," he said, thumping his fist on the table and making Francesca jump. "As if the *Augustina* had run aground in open ocean. Up the thing comes, oozing onto the aft deck, ripping and tearing oak beams like twigs. Tentacles rose into the sky—"

"Wh, what was it?" interrupted Francesca.

"Oh, a kraken, to be sure. A monster squid that eats ships."

Antonio leaned forward with a half-smile. "And how long would you say the tentacles were?"

"Forty feet at the least!" Fredrico exclaimed stretching out his arms.

Francesca felt as if a tentacle had wrapped around her chest and squeezed, her breathing shallow. Antonio put his hands over his mouth.

Fredrico continued. "It seemed as though there were a hundred sinuous limbs." He held his hands curled, one above the other as though wielding a two-handed axe. "We fought like lions, me with my sword and ax, my crew with pistols and muskets and any manner of weapon."

He shook his head sadly. "Men were seized by those snaking tentacles and stuffed into the beast's maw, weapons and all."

Antonio got up and turned away with his hands to his face. Fredrico glared at him, then leaned toward Francesca. "Well, young sir, we battled for hours. We lost a dozen men, and nearly the *Augustina* as well—the creature rending it like a paper toy. Our quartermaster, well, two tentacles grabbed him at both ends and played tug o' war. No one deserves to go out like that."

Fredrico fell silent shaking his head and Francesca listened to her own ragged breathing. Antonio and Fredrico watched her. Finally, she tore her eyes from Fredrico's face and took another drink.

"We killed it in the end," he said. "But it was a near thing. After that, I came here to work in this bar, a goodly distance from the ocean."

"That is quite the tale," said Antonio from behind his cup.

"Indeed." Fredrico rubbed his jaw. "The kraken used to just live in Australian waters, but now that I think of it, I've heard from old crewmates that the damn things are turning up everywhere nowadays."

Antonio raised his tankard to Fredrico. "I think you made the right choice coming here. I know I would be frightened out of my skin to go to sea with those monsters lurking out there, but Signore Dampier here is made of sterner stuff. I'm sure he's not afraid."

Francesca nodded vaguely. She felt sick to her stomach and a little dizzy.

Fredrico leaned back. "You know, these things are cyclical. The creatures multiply like crazy and then die off in masse. In a couple years the seas will most likely be safe again." He looked at Francesca. "Seems a shame to risk your hide, when in a couple years you could sail to Australia without a worry in the world."

"I guess discretion is the better part of valor, as my father likes to say," said Antonio.

Francesca slumped, elbows on the table, staring into her cup. Now the world, which had seemed so full of bright, shining adventure, instead seemed full of dark monsters sliding just under the surface. She wanted to be home, in the garden with Nana or curled on her bed with a book. She ran a hand through her shaggy hair. *But how can I go home?* How would she explain her hair? *I'll be in so much trouble.* She felt tears forming and scrunched her eyes shut. *Boys don't cry.* She took a long drink to hide her trembling chin and lips.

Fredrico looked a little sad as he stood. "I'll let you lads chat." He headed back to the bar as a man shuffled up to it.

Antonio and Francesca were quiet for a while as Francesca fought to control her disappointment. Finally, Antonio said. "I still think you're very brave."

She gave a half laugh, half cry. She didn't feel very brave. She felt like a failure.

"I'm serious," said Antonio. "You were willing to go, despite the pirates and the storms and shipwrecks and all. That shows you have courage. Going despite the krakens would just show that you're crazy."

She gave a weak laugh. "I'm not crazy. I don't want to get pulled in half and eaten."

He shrugged. "I just want you to know, I'd be proud to have a brother like you."

She looked up at him and fought back new tears. Then she looked around at the taverna and asked, "So, have you been here before?"

"A couple times on a dare, and with some of the older boys from... my father's fencing school."

"And that girl you were with, why were you giving her a ride?"

Antonio flushed and put his face in his mug, drinking deeply. Then he wiped his lips with his cuff and shrugged. "She's pretty. I like her."

"I thought you said girls are a pain."

He nodded then smiled. "Maybe I'm changing my mind. Some are alright. I like my sister. She's smart, and brave, and never backs down from a fight. You remind me a little of her."

Francesca pulled some of her hair down over her face. "Yuck. Who wants to be a girl."

Antonio laughed. "Not me. It seems difficult. They're always in trouble for something. But my sister takes her punishment well, because she knows our family still loves her."

She looked at him sideways. "Does she know that?"

"I hope so. My brother teases her a lot, but he doesn't mean anything by it. It's just his way. And my father over protects her because she reminds him of our mother who died. I hope she understands."

Francesca swirled her beer around in her mug. She couldn't remember ever talking with Antonio this much. It felt nice. "And what about you?"

"Well, I guess I've been busy with my friends. I haven't spent much time with my sister. That's my fault. I should make up for that. Maybe I could go for a ride with her."

"I bet she would like that."

They both fell silent and sipped their drinks. A man off to her right belched loudly.

"So, what will you do now, Signore Dampier?" asked Antonio.

Francesca sighed deeply and stood up. The room seemed to sway a little bit around her, and she held on to the table. "I'll go home, I guess, and take what comes." She could see her governess' horrified face in her mind. This would be bad.

Antonio laughed, "It's a good thing that Horse knows the way. You drank a lot of ale. And don't worry too much. I'm sure adventure is just around the corner."

"Do you think so?" She hoped he was right. "What about you? What will you do?"

"I guess I'll head home too. After I finish my ale."

Francesca nodded. That was perfect. Signore Dampier couldn't very well ride home with Antonio. "Goodbye, Signore DiCesare, it has been nice talking with you."

Antonio raised a hand as Francesca tottered toward the door. "Safe travels."

I wish, thought Francesa as she untied Achilles and climbed onto his back. "Let's go home, Horse."

Achilles tossed his head and turned toward home.

FRANCESCA AND THE BARON'S SON

Tuscany
May 1st, 1711

Francesca could tell that the bride had been crying, and they weren't tears of joy. Her eyes and nose looked red and sore.

The bride, Francesca's eighteen-year-old cousin, wore a golden brocade dress that tapered to her cinched waist and exploded into voluminous skirts. The elegant dress only accentuated the girl's plainness. She had mousy brown hair and a long pale face. The groom, about the same age, looked angry, but his weak chin suggested an air of peevishness.

An old bishop in white robes and a tall miter hat stretched his hands over the couple, speaking in Latin. His words echoed around the small stone chapel. Light from a stained-glass window colored the hem of the bishop's robe and a dozen candles softened the gloom.

Francesca fidgeted.

She was a girl of eleven with impatient green eyes, the color of a deep forest glen. Suntanned skin nearly hid the dusting of freckles across the bridge of her nose. Her auburn hair had been swept into a knot at her nape, but much of it had fallen loose. She wore a green dress that matched her eyes, except for the smudges of brown over her knees.

Francesca's eyes searched the room for something to occupy her. She kicked her feet absently, and Papa, seated on her left, took her hand. That was his way of telling her to settle down. She tried, but she was annoyed. He had said that her cousin's wedding would be a happy occasion, but no one seemed happy, and it seemed to be taking forever.

With her fingertip, she traced the scars that crisscrossed the back of Papa's hand, remnants from his days as a soldier and duelist. He smiled down at her, crinkling his steel-grey eyes. He squeezed her hand, then turned his attention back to the bishop.

Francesca gazed around at the other children. Past her father sat her older brothers, Antonio and Sebastian. Sebi caught her eye and stuck out his tongue. She returned the gesture. Papa scowled at them both.

In the pew in front of them sat Francesca's nine-year-old twin cousins, Camella and Gabriela. Camella always wore pink and Gabriela blue so that people could tell them apart. Their sister stood before the bishop fighting back tears. Francesca tried unsuccessfully to get their attention. Papa had promised that they could play after the ceremony, and she wanted to spend time with them.

The only other child was the younger brother of the groom, Bencino. He sat between his parents, the baron and baroness. He had brooding eyes, like the groom, and his lips seemed stuck in a permanent sneer, or maybe that was just his face.

The bishop ceased his droning and the unhappy couple turned and marched solemnly out of the chapel. The Baron and his wife followed, then her cousins and their parents. Francesca and her family followed along with a few other guests.

Bencino must have stayed behind. He came up behind them, shoving Antonio roughly out of the way as he passed. Antonio, five inches taller and a few years older than Bencino, started after him, but Papa put a restraining hand on Antonio's shoulder. Antonio turned and Papa gave him a small but firm shake of the head. Antonio's jaws clenched but he held his place. The boy had noble blood and her family, while wealthy and successful, did not.

The chapel occupied a small hill close to the rambling, utilitarian manor that belonged to Francesca's uncle. The ungainly stone house seemed out of place in the miles of spring green pastures that stretched up into the foothills blushing with red poppies. The soft cream bodies of sheep dotted the hillsides, half of them looking naked after the spring shearing. Lines of evenly spaced cypress trees followed a distant road.

Back at the manor, Camella and Gabriela's governess led them and Francesca to the upstairs playroom. Tapestries draped the walls in domestic scenes in pale blues and greens. A small fire crackled in the white marble fireplace, but the window opened to the fresh air. An ebony piano sat in one corner, dark and imposing in the pale room. The governess retreated to a pastel floral chair, retrieving her needlework from a bag at her feet.

Francesca turned to her cousins with an excited bounce. "What shall we play?"

"Let's have tea," said Camella, sitting down at a child-sized table spread with a child-sized tea set.

Francesca's forehead creased. She'd had enough of sitting still.

Gabriela pressed a doll into Francesca's arms and picked one up for herself that wore a dress that matched hers. Camella put a doll in another chair and pretended to spoon-feed it.

Francesca examined the doll in her arms. It was a decent likeness of a baby, carved of wood with painted features, glued on hair, and a white gown. "What should I do with it?"

Gabriela gave her a puzzled look. "Play with it."

Francesca tossed the doll in the air, catching it by one arm.

"No!" cried her cousins in unison.

Gabriela pressed the doll back into her arms. "You have to take care of it." She smoothed its tangled hair. "Don't you have dolls at home?"

Francesca nodded as she pictured her dolls, stacked in a corner and covered with dust. She watched the happiness on Gabriela's face as she hummed and rocked her doll.

Camella scolded her doll cheerfully while spooning it imaginary food. "You must eat, or you'll grow up plain and no one will want to marry you."

Francesca rocked her doll and poked at its painted eyes. She didn't understand how this was supposed to be fun. "I think mine is broken." She set the doll on the table and turned to look around the room examining one bookcase filled with games and musical instruments. "Do you have any books?"

Camella shook her head. "No. We don't read. Papa says it ruins a girl."

"You mean you don't, or you don't know how?" asked Francesca.

"Mama wanted us to learn, but Papa said we couldn't," Camella replied.

Francesca shook her head in amazement. "But…" She stopped, not quite sure what she had meant to ask. It seemed so odd. Papa insisted that she read not only Italian, but English and Latin as well. She wandered to the open window. A warm breeze brought in the earthy smell of sheep pastures. A pond captured a bit of sky and glowed like a turquoise gem in a deep green setting. Her brothers raced along the trail to the woods.

Jealousy wiggled through Francesca's stomach; the airy room suddenly seemed close and confining.

"Could we go play by the pond?" Francesca asked.

"Why?" said Gabriela.

"We might fall in!" said Camella.

"Certainly not," said the governess straightening her high-necked, charcoal grey dress. "But—"

A light knock on the door interrupted her. A servant girl leaned in. "Excuse me, Mancare Ricci. The mistress would like to speak with you."

"Very well." The governess carefully folded her needlework and set it back in her bag. She rose, smoothing her skirts, and turned to the girls. "But you may ask the cook for a basket and have a picnic in the garden."

Francesca's cousins grinned with excitement. Francesca gave them a weak smile.

"Just be careful not to muss your dresses," said the governess. "I'll join you there."

They all headed out of the room.

The hallways were whitewashed plaster punctuated by dark beams. Francesca followed her cousins, but paused at a partly open door when she heard Papa and her uncle talking inside. The others hurried on, but she peeked in. The dark paneled room had one whole wall of bookshelves and a fire sputtered in the brick fireplace.

"Let them wait for their dinner," said her uncle Tino, a robust man with a face much like Papa's except tending to flab in the jowls. His face was red, and he sipped amber fluid from a crystal glass. "Serves them right for treating us like the poor relations."

"But you feel it's a good match," said Papa. There was a question in the way he said it.

Her uncle nodded. "Better than I had hoped for. Mind you, we had to settle an extensive dowry on the girl. And even then, it wouldn't have happened if the baron hadn't gambled away his holdings."

"I just meant that neither of them looked..." he searched for words, "keen on the match."

Uncle Tino's uproarious laughter startled Francesca. Then her uncle saw Papa's serious expression and the laughter faded. He took a sip of his drink. "I forgot who I was talking to. Thurio DiCesare, the only man in Tuscany who married for love." The derision he put into the word *love* was clear.

Papa frowned.

Uncle Tino swallowed the rest of his drink. "For twenty years the baron's been treating me like chaff. Well, no more! All he owns is now because of me, and my grandchildren's blood will be as blue as his." He threw the glass into the fireplace.

The shattering sound roused Francesca and she shivered as she hurried down the hall after the girls. Now she understood why the bride had been crying.

———————

The formal gardens behind the house were set on a grid, four squares of grass intersected by wide, raked gravel walks. Sharp rectangle hedges of boxwood and regimented flowers in neat beds edged the walkways. Even the red poppies that grew haphazardly on the hillsides were here evenly spaced and upright. At least a wisteria that covered the arbor at the center of the garden twisted wildly up the beams and bloomed in lavender abandon.

Camella and Gabriela spread a cream-colored blanket on the closest square of grass and arranged utensils, plates, and napkins. They knelt on the corners of the blanket staring when Francesca plopped down cross-legged.

Camella took bread, cheese, and oranges from the basket as Gabriela poured tea. Her hand stopped, mid-pour, as they heard horse hooves crunching on the gravel walk. The twins turned to see who approached. Francesca noticed their bodies tense when the baron's young son, Bencino, rode into view. The girls held motionless, only their eyes moving, like rabbits hoping to be passed over by a hawk.

But the hawk spotted them.

Bencino rode a dappled grey horse. A riding crop dangled from a strap around his wrist. He grinned at them, but there was no warmth in his expression. He turned his horse toward them. Camella and Gabriela rose, backing away. They curtsied quickly and awkwardly, still backing.

45

Francesca stood as Bencino urged the horse between the hedges and onto the grass. Francesca looked uncertainly from the boy to the frightened girls who moved toward the far side of the square. Camella beckoned to her. Francesca looked again at Bencino, wondering what they were afraid of. He was not much taller than her, thin and angular.

Francesca curtsied as he approached. "Good day, my Lord."

She glanced over her shoulder. Her cousins had slipped around the far hedge and stood watching from behind it.

Bencino ignored Francesca. He rode straight toward their blanket. His horse paused at the edge and shook its head. The boy dug his heels into the horse's side, urging it on. It snorted but took a step onto the blanket.

Francesca grabbed the bridle. "Please, stop, my Lord, you'll break everything."

The horse paused.

Bencino looked at Francesca. "Let go." His voice was cold.

"But, my Lord, our tea."

The boy's riding crop whipped out and stung the back of Francesca's hand. She snatched back her hand with a muffled yelp. She stared at Bencino in disbelief.

He whipped his crop against the horse's side, and it started forward onto the blanket. A teacup and saucer crunched beneath an ironclad hoof.

Anger surged through Francesca. She shoved at the horse's hind quarter trying to move it off the blanket, but Bencino reined the horse in, and it turned in a circle, oranges, tiny sandwiches, cookies, and plates crushed beneath its feet.

"Stop!" yelled Francesca.

Bencino laughed.

From behind her, Francesca heard the governess' voice. She sounded frightened as well. "Girls, come here."

Camella and Gabriela hurried along the gravel path toward the governess.

Francesca turned to the woman. "Stop him!"

The governess scowled. "Francesca, come away from there."

Then Francesca felt the bite of the riding crop on her bare neck, like the sting of a dozen wasps.

She put a hand to her neck and turned toward Bencino with rage clouding her vision. She reached up, grabbed the riding crop, and pulled. The crop's strap was wrapped around the boy's wrist. They struggled for a moment, then the horse reared.

Bencino slid out of the saddle. He fell with a thud onto the ground next to the blanket. The horse pranced away.

The governess and the girls stared with their hands over their mouths.

The boy rose to his feet, glaring. "Do you know who I am?" he demanded.

Francesca balled her fists. "A coward, if you bully little girls and break their things."

He swung the crop again, stinging Francesca's cheek and raising a red welt. She tasted blood where her cheek had hit her teeth.

Bencino never saw Francesca's fist coming. He staggered backwards, tripped on the tangled blanket, and fell. Blood poured from his nose. The governess and the girls let out strangled gasps.

Francesca shook out her hand, then crossed her arms.

After a dazed moment the boy rose. He wiped his sleeve across his bloody face. "You'll pay for this!" He turned and marched toward his horse which nibbled at the boxwood hedge. "Wait 'til I tell my father."

"Yes, I hope you do," said Francesca. "I'm sure the baron will be happy to hear that his son was beaten by a little girl."

Bencino stopped in his tracks. He turned and glowered at Francesca, his face turning red. Then he continued toward his horse, though much less purposefully. He climbed into the saddle and gathered the reins. Aiming the horse directly at Francesca, he whipped the crop against the horse's hindquarters.

Francesca jumped out of the way as the horse barreled past her and leapt over the hedge.

Camella and Gabriela ran to Francesca who frowned as she surveyed the ruins of their tea.

"Why didn't you run away?" said Camella.

"Why should I? It's our tea."

"But he's the baron's son," said Camella nervously plucking at her skirt.

"That doesn't give him the right to frighten you and break your things."

"Yes, it does," said Gabriella with a slight shiver.

The governess came and stood behind the twins. "The baron would be within his rights to confiscate all this land."

"Over a bloody nose?" said Francesca.

"Over an assault on his son."

The fire drained from her veins and a cold ball grew in her stomach. "He, he, wouldn't."

When the governess marched Francesca and the twins inside, they found Papa and Uncle Tino still in the den. Papa saw Francesca's red welts that were quickly bruising and stormed off, calling for the baron. Uncle Tino caught him before he'd gone far and directed Papa through a doorway and closed the door. Francesca could hear both men yelling from inside.

Papa and Uncle emerged a few minutes later calmer, but with red faces. Papa took a deep breath, then turned to Uncle Tino. "I expect it's time we headed home."

Uncle Tino nodded. "I'll send someone to find your boys."

As the group made their way to the front door, the baron appeared from the dining room. He was taller than Papa, thin and effeminate, but his eyes burned. "So, this is the girl," he said, heading for Francesca.

"Yes, my lord," said Uncle Tino. "They were just leaving. The maestro wishes to get her home so he can punish her privately."

Francesca resisted the urge to back away as the baron approached. Her heart pounded.

The baron grabbed her chin with finger and thumb and tilted her face roughly to see her bruised cheek and neck. "And severely, I trust."

Out of the corner of her eye Francesca saw Papa start forward, then check himself. "Of course, my Lord."

The baron released her face with a slight shove and looked at Uncle Tino. "Then we'll speak no more of this." He turned and left.

Everyone but Francesca seemed to deflate as they let out their breath.

Shadows were beginning to lengthen as they stepped outside. Already their carriage, a covered post-chaise with a tan body with black trim, waited. Antonio and Sebastian approached along the path to the woods.

"I'll send along your things," said Uncle Tino. Then he took the maestro's arm. "The girl's a menace, Thurio. She's practically feral."

"Not true."

"You spoil her."

"I treat her exactly like her brothers."

"That's precisely my point."

The children climbed in, Francesca and Antonio taking the seats facing backwards and Sebastian facing forward, leaving a space for Papa.

Papa and Uncle Tino spoke beside the carriage, Uncle's face earnest. "I can imagine how difficult it is to raise a girl without a mother, but you do her no favors by treating her like her brothers. How is she to learn her place?"

Uncle Tino paused. Then he linked his arm with the maestro and turned him so that they were facing away from the carriage. He dropped his voice. "Take her home. Give her a good thrashing. Knock the spirit out of her. Teach her that she's nothing, for if you don't do it with love, someone else will do it with malice." He shook his head. "No one will have her to wife this way. She'll be good for nothing but the convent."

"I appreciate your concern," said the maestro. "Goodbye, Tino." He nodded to the driver as he climbed in, and they headed down the driveway.

Francesca sat opposite Papa. She looked at him, but he avoided her eyes. They were quiet as the carriage turned out of the long, curved driveway onto the road.

Sebastian giggled. "We heard that Francesca beat up a baron."

The maestro's eyes flashed to Francesca, and they were full of deep sorrow. "It's no laughing matter. The baron could have brought charges or had her flogged."

"But then he'd have to admit in public that a girl beat up his son," said Antonio.

"Did I do wrong, Papa?" asked Francesca. "You always say that it's honorable for the strong to protect the weak."

Papa leaned forward and put his head in his hands.

"You're supposed to *be* the weak, idiot," said Antonio.

"Hush," said Papa.

"Why?" said Francesca. "I'm stronger than Camella and Gabriela. Shouldn't I protect them?"

"I wish it were that simple," said Papa.

"Why can Bencino be a bully just because his father is a baron? It's not right."

The maestro looked up and laid a gentle hand on Francesca's bruised cheek. "No, it's not." He leaned back, his voice becoming stern. "But actions have consequences. You're confined to your room for a week."

Francesca frowned. She knew better than to argue and turn her punishment into two weeks. She stared angrily out the window at the cypress trees passing by. *I was in the right. I know I was. Why should I be punished? It's not fair. Actions only have consequences for some*, she thought.

She had hated seeing the twins so frightened by Bencino. It was worse to see Papa and Uncle afraid of the baron. Papa was worth a hundred barons. It made her angry to the very core of her being. She didn't care about the sting of her welts, or the week in her room. It was worth it to see justice done, if only briefly.

She was right, and she'd do it again if she had to.

CATALINA COMES TO THE SALLE

Dear Diary,

I don't know why I'm writing this, except that Nana gave you to me and you're very beautiful, so I thought I had better use you. I don't want to be ungrateful. Nana said to put down my thoughts and feelings, so...

Nana and Papa told me at dinner tonight that I'm going to get a companion tomorrow. I don't know what to think. It seems a little odd. Usually, it's old ladies who get companions, not twelve-year-old girls like me. Why do I have to have one? And how do you just give someone a person? What if I don't like her? Can I give her back? What if she's just a spy for the grownups?

I can't let them find out about my fencing, or my jumping Achilles over hedges, or my tree climbing. I won't be able to do *anything* around this new girl. Honestly, it's like having *another* governess when one is already too many.

Nana says that there are too many boys around the villa, and I need a feminine influence. Papa says I spend too much time alone.

But I like being alone. Then I can do what *I* want, not what they want me to do. What's so great about a feminine influence anyway?

The real reason they're doing this is because last year I punched the baron's son, and then, there's Geno. But Geno was hurting that cat on purpose, no matter what he said afterwards. And I warned him to stop, and he wouldn't. Some people just need a good sock on the nose.

Though after a week confined to my room, my hand still hurts from that punch.

Anyway, we'll see what this new girl is like tomorrow.

Goodnight, Diary.

August 13th, 1712

Dear Diary,

I hate her.

Her name is Catalina. She showed up in a fancy silk dress with her pretty face and her long dark hair. She cried almost all day, saying she missed her mother. Then she looked at me like it was my fault! How is it my fault? I don't even want her here.

Nana tried to cheer Catalina up and spent almost all afternoon showing her around and helping her decorate her new room. Nana hardly said two words to me all day. How is this supposed to be more of a feminine influence when now I don't even get to talk with Nana anymore?

It looks like Catalina is going to be eating with us in the family dining room too. Sebi and Antonio spent all dinner staring at her like idiots. Yes, she's very pretty, but so what. She doesn't know the first thing about fencing or horses.

So how do I get rid of her? Any suggestions?

I thought not.

You are no help, Diary.

August 13th 1712

Dearest Mamma,

I know you told me to be strong, so I'm trying hard not to cry, but I can't help it. I know my being here is good for my education and for Enzo's. I know that this will help Enzo's career, but I miss you and I wish I could come home.

Grandmother DiCesare, (Nana, as she asked me to call her) has been very kind. This morning when I arrived, she showed me all around the villa, which is very lovely, especially the silk drapes. Every time I complimented a piece of art or a decoration, she had the servants take it down and carry it to my room. We spent the afternoon decorating my room and she did her best to make me feel welcome. I like her very much. She can't walk very well, but she has a dry, sharp sense of humor that I think you would enjoy.

I had dinner with Maestro DiCesare, Nana, the two sons, Antonio and Sebastian, and Francesca. Everyone was kind, but it felt awkward. Antonio, who is sixteen, and Sebastian, who is fourteen, both stared as if they'd never seen a girl before. The maestro didn't exactly interrogate me, but he did ask a lot of questions about my education and habits. I think it was his way of showing interest and getting to know me. I expect it works fine with boys, but I wanted to crawl under the table.

And Francesca, what can I say about her? This girl I'm supposed to be a friend to. Although never rude, neither was she welcoming. It's clear that none of this was her idea. If anything, she seems suspicious of me. I don't know what it is that she thinks I'm likely to do.

While Nana gave me the tour, she followed behind, saying next to nothing. Papa would have told her to stop moping. While Nana and I decorated my room she seemed both bored and restless. She spent the entire time watching the students who were learning to fence in the courtyard below, hardly paying any attention to me and Nana. She said very little. I can't tell if she's shy, or just not interested in talking to me.

I know she's two years younger than me, and I'll need to be patient. Nana took me aside and said as much. But I really don't understand this girl. She doesn't seem to want to talk about anything but fencing or horses.

What if she doesn't like me? What if I don't' like her? Does that mean I can come home? I miss you all so much.

Thinking of you,

Your loving Catalina

August 14ᵗʰ 1712

Dear Diary,

Catalina almost caught me fencing in my room this morning. She knocked on my door during fencing class while I worked on my low line parries. I barely managed to stuff everything under the bed before she opened the door. It was <u>so</u> close! Now I'm sure she's a spy. I'm going to have to start locking my door during class.

She offered to do my hair, which I had already combed and tied back. Why would I want some fancy hairdo that means I can't move my head all day? I may have laughed in her face, which probably wasn't very nice, but honestly!

She asked if I wanted to do anything fun today, so I suggested we go for a ride. "Oh, no." she said. "I won't go near one of those beasts!" Can you believe it? Afraid of horses! She doesn't even ride! I asked what she does for fun, and she said she sews and plays card games. Sews! For fun! A spy *and* crazy.

I got stuck spending the afternoon playing Briscola with her, Nana, and Signora Álvarez. The signora gushed over her dress, and her 'deportment' telling me I should take note. Great. Yet more things for the signora to lecture me about. Thank you so much, Catalina!

At least I won three rounds and captured the Briscola card twice, so maybe some of it was fun, but not nearly as much fun as jumping Achilles over the hedges.

At dinner Sebi and Antonio acted like idiots, trying to impress her. They nearly fell over each other to hold her chair and to pass her the potatoes or the salt. I was so embarrassed!

This evening, I asked if she reads, and she said she did. Thank God, I thought, at least that's something we have in common. But it turns out she only reads those silly pastorals like *Cassandre* where some handsome, but not very bright hero mopes after some useless lady who does nothing but slurp tea and will barely speak to him. How can anyone read that nonsense?

I tried to loan her Dampier's book about his trip to the New World, but she looked at it like it was a snake that might bite her. At least that's a book about something real and interesting!

Afterwards I pretended to be tired so I could get away from her and she gave me *such* a look!

How do I get rid of her? Thoughts? Suggestions?

Goodnight Diary.

August 15th, 1712

Dearest Mamma,

Please get me out of here!

Francesca is impossible! The girl can't sit still for more than two minutes. She has to be constantly *doing* something. Preferably something that she's been told *not* to do. First, she wanted to ride horses, then trudge through the woods, then chase rabbits with one of the hounds, I hope she was joking when she mentioned climbing trees! Then she gets angry when I say no, as if I'm the unreasonable one.

She could be a pretty girl if she put in the least effort. Instead, she wears plain linen dresses, pulls her hair back in a ponytail, and is brown from riding her horse daily. I suggested she wear a hat to keep her skin fair and she looked at me as though I had suggested she take her head off and leave it behind.

Her brother told me that the reason I'm here is because last week she punched a boy. She hit him right in the face! She's quite insane! If she tries to hit me, I'm coming home no matter what.

After dinner Signora Álvarez told us that she is leaving next week to go take care of her sick mother in Cascina. She'll be gone indefinitely. The poor dear thing. I hope her mother recovers, but it doesn't sound likely.

The signora has been kind for the most part, if a bit critical. I'll be sorry to see her go and leave me here with her.

When can I come home to visit?

Love,

Catalina

August 15th, 1712

Dear Diary,

Signora Álvarez is leaving. She must be relieved. She's criticized everyone and everything around here for the last two years. I'm happy, but also a bit worried. Nana likes to say, "Better the devil you know than the devil you don't." Still, how could a new governess be any worse?

Now I just need to figure out how to get a new companion. One that doesn't just sit around all the time doing boring sewing and reading boring books. She never wants to *do* anything. I suggested an outdoor activity might put some color in her cheeks and she looked at me as if I'd suggested a swim in a lake of lava.

Nana lectured me again about making friends with Catalina. Well, they can make me sit around with her, but they can't make me like her.

Goodnight, Diary.

August 18th, 1712

Dearest Mamma,

I lost my head today. I was so angry with her.

For the last few days, whenever we're not in class, she locks herself in her room or gallops off on her horse, so she doesn't have to spend time with me. I'm supposed to be her companion, but she makes it impossible! If things keep up like this, Enzo and I will be sent home, and while I would love to be home, I don't want to ruin Enzo's future because this infuriating girl won't talk to me.

Today, I saw her sneaking into the house with grass stains all down one side of her dress. When I mentioned it, she accused me of being a spy, for heaven's sake! I, of course, said that was ridiculous, but she wanted me to prove it. How do you prove you are _not_ something?

Anyway, we shouted at each other until Nana came and sent us both to our rooms. I was so ashamed of myself.

I expect I may be home tomorrow. I'm afraid I've failed our whole family.

Missing you,

Your loving Catalina

August 18th, 1712

Dear Diary,

I hate her, I hate her, I hate her.

Today a fox spooked Achilles while we were jumping the fallen log in the sheep pasture, and I spilled and slid halfway down the hill. I snuck back with a twisted knee, limping, and the first thing Catalina says is "You'll never get those grass stains out."

I was mad, so I said, "Thank you so much for your concern *for my dress*. I can see why you're such a good companion." Then she said something about how would I know if she's a good companion when I keep avoiding her. I told her she should go spy on someone else. She claims she's not a spy, as any spy would.

Anyway, with all the shouting, Nana found out about the dress and confined me to my room all day tomorrow. Thank you so much, Catalina. At least she got sent to her room as well.

And, I've got my revenge. I found a way to get rid of her. While Nana was out in the garden I snuck into her room and borrowed her favorite necklace (the one with the cameo of my mother) and hid it among Catalina's stockings. Now it is just a matter of time before Nana misses it and the search begins. Catalina will be sent home in disgrace not long after.

I can't wait to be on my own again.

In the meantime, I guess you and I are spending the day together, Diary.

August 23ʳᵈ, 1712

Dearest Mamma,

A new governess arrived today with nothing but a small satchel. Her name is Signora Bianchi. And so far, I don't much care for the woman. Where Signora Alvarez was pudgy and round, this woman is rail thin and very sever in her dress and hairstyle. She makes Francesca, who dresses very simply, look positively lavish by comparison.

The first thing she did was take all the art and decoration out of her new room, (Signora Alvarez's old room) and leave up just one crucifix on the wall. She says that art and decoration are merely distractions from one's duty. I didn't like the sound of that! So, not an art lover.

Then she asked all sorts of questions about our education. Worst of all, she took away my books! She said that pastorals fill girls' heads with unrealistic ideas about romance and that she discourages reading in ladies in general since it distracts them from their duties. Just what duties is she talking about? I'm worried.

Francesca didn't even get to meet her today since she was confined to her room for one thing or another. Not a great first impression, I'm sure.

I miss you more and more,

Love,

Catalina

August 25th, 1712

Dear Diary,

How do I get Signora Alvarez back? This devil I didn't know is indeed much worse!

First, Signora Bianchi tried to forbid me to ride Achilles!

Well, I couldn't let that stand. I went straight to Papa, who sided with me. He said it was good for my constitution to go for a ride regularly. She had some foolhardy notion that it would make me barren, which Papa dismissed out of hand, looking rather embarrassed about the whole thing.

Then, she tried to take my books. When I pointed out that they were Papa's books and that my brothers had both read them, and that they were teaching me geography, she eventually relented. But not before ordering me to spend a day working in the kitchen as punishment for arguing with her. Honestly!

She has our entire day scheduled now. From sunup to sundown, if we're not in class, Catalina and I are scheduled to be either spinning and carding wool, or sewing, or praying, or doing our schoolwork. We don't have ten minutes to ourselves. How am I supposed to practice my fencing? Why do we have to work all day?

I've complained to Papa and Nana, but they just say that every governess has her methods and that I should give her a chance. A chance to do what, work us to death? Or worse, bore us to death?

Nana asked if I had seen her necklace today. I said no. In a few days I'll mention that I might have seen Catalina with it.

Goodnight, Diary

August 30th 1712

Dearest Mamma,

I know I've complained about Francesca, but at least she has a sense of humor. Signora Bianchi does not. Not at all, as far as I can tell. It's been over a week, and I have yet to see her laugh, or even smile for that matter. She prays, she lectures about duty, and she orders us about. Yesterday I was humming as I sewed, and she reprimanded me.

She and Francesca are constantly bickering, like two billy goats butting horns. And while Francesca may occasionally deserve punishment, Signora Bianchi seems to enjoy inflicting it over petty things. I almost admire Francesca's tenacity in fighting back. Almost. I would, if she weren't just making it harder for both of us.

I've had just about enough of this woman, and I think I might do something drastic. If she can be petty, so can I. At least it will make me feel better.

Sending all my love,

Catalina.

August 31st 1712

Dear Diary,

Today was the best day ever. Well, the second best. The best will be the day Signora Bianchi leaves for good. But today was special.

First off, tired of the signora making us spin wool every day, I got up last night and did a little *maintenance* on the spinning wheel. I took the wheel apart and replaced the bolt in the hub of the wheel with a shorter one.

When Catalina and I finished our history lesson we were assigned to meet the signora in the sewing room. For once, I was eager to go. It worked out perfectly. She had just sat down at the spinning wheel when we entered.

As we took our seats to work on repairing the salle's napkins, the signora threaded the yarn and put her foot on the treadle. I held my breath, watching. She worked the pedals and the wheel started to spin as she fed the wool into her yarn. She had a few yards of new yarn on the bobbin when the wheel started to wobble, then, to my delight, it came loose, spun off across the floor and out of the room and down the hallway, dragging the bobbin, unrolling behind it.

I tried my best to keep from laughing, but I heard Catalina snort with laughter, and I gave in, fits of laughter making my sides ache.

You should have seen the signora's purple face as she chased after the wheel. Catalina looked at me and raised an eyebrow, asking if I did it, and I gave her a nod.

Once the signora had caught the wheel, rerolled all her yarn, and examined the bolt, she demanded to know who had done this. We both played innocent perfectly. With no damning evidence, she was forced to merely punish us for laughing with three more hours of kitchen duty. Ha! We can do that in our sleep.

But the fun wasn't over yet. Unable to do her spinning, the signora pulled out her knitting. Catalina gave me a wink and a head nod toward our governess. I watched from the corner of my eye as I sewed.

Signora Bianchi seemed to be having difficulties. The needles kept slipping from her fingers, gliding through her knitting, and falling onto the floor. She picked them up and examined them, started again and the same thing happened.

I raised an eyebrow to Catalina, and she gave me a nod. She mouthed the words *duck fat*.

The signora tried three or four more times as Catalina and I tried our very best not to laugh. Catalina's face turned bright red, and her sides shook. I'm sure I looked much the same as I bit my lip to stop the giggles.

Eventually she gave it up, put away her knitting, and pulled out her needle and thread. I looked at Catalina, and she gave me a wicked smile. Sure enough, Catalina had greased that needle too. Every time the signora tried to pull the thread the needle squirted out of her fingertips.

We both had to fake coughing spells to cover our laughter and the signora huffed and told us to go get a drink of water.

We made it halfway down the stairs before we fell into each other's arms in hysterics.

Catalina is the best companion ever. I'm sorry I doubted her. I can't wait to see her in the morning. Tomorrow I need to put Nana's necklace back where it belongs.

Good night, Diary.

September 1st, 1712

Dearest Mamma,

This afternoon, I came into my room after lunch and caught Francesca digging through my stocking drawer. I was annoyed, but we were doing so well together after yesterday's pranks, I didn't want to spoil the mood, so I didn't yell at her. She didn't hear me open the door, so I just leaned against the frame and said, "If you need stockings, just ask."

To be honest, I expected some excuse, or denial, but she looked at me, the corners of her mouth twitched down, she looked thoroughly miserable, and she started to cry. She's always been so fierce, that tears were the last thing I expected. Then she held up a gold chain with a cameo hanging from it. She said, "I'm so sorry Catalina, I've been so awful to you! You should hate me."

I was confused as she sat down on my bed and put her face in her hands. It wasn't my necklace, so she wasn't stealing from me. Was she giving me a necklace? Then I realized. Heat flashed through me and I said, "You're trying to make me out to be a thief, aren't you!"

She shook her head and wiped at her tears and said, "Yesterday I was, today I was trying to undo it." She looked up at me with those bright emerald eyes. "I'm sorry Catalina, I thought you were like all the rest of them."

I didn't understand. "The rest of who?" I asked.

"All of them. Everyone. All the people who are constantly watching me, lecturing me, scolding me, punishing me. All the people who want me to be anyone other than who I am." The hope in her eyes caught my breath as she said, "But you're not them. You're on my side."

That was when I realized how terribly alone she has always felt. Why she's constantly fighting the whole world. Why she's always so fierce, and how strong she is to never give in, or give up and be who they want her to be. Maybe things would have been different if her mother hadn't died. Maybe then she would have been someone else, someone who wanted what the world wanted of her. Who knows.

But this afternoon, I realized that I couldn't give her a mother's love, but I could give her a big sister's. I told her, "They may have brought me here, but they brought me here <u>for you</u>. I'm on your side, Francesca, always."

Well, the hug she gave me nearly broke my ribs. I guess she loves just as fiercely as she fights. So, I guess this time, I'm not hoping or asking to come home. Francesca needs me, and this is where I belong.

Love,

Your Catalina

NEXT UP IN THE LADY BLADE SERIES: THE MAESTRO'S DAUGHTER

The Maestro's Daughter tells the story of Francesca, her friend Catalina, and her family and household at the famed fencing school, Salle DiCesare. It begins when Francesca is sixteen. Francesca watches from the shadows as her father trains noble sons in the art of the blade. But in a world where swords belong to men, her dream of becoming a fencer is impossible—unless she seizes it for herself.

When a handsome, young English noble arrives at her father's school, Francesca finds the perfect opportunity. In secret, she strikes a dangerous bargain; lessons by moonlight in exchange for a forbidden friendship.

But defiance, secrecy, and forbidden love have their price, especially for young women, and the punishment often outweighs the crime. Things come to a head when an unwanted arranged marriage, and Francesca's manipulations, bring an avalanche of consequences for everyone.

Faced with the weight of her choices, Francesca must decide whether to bow to the world's rules or carve her own path—one forged in steel and sacrifice.

ABOUT THE AUTHOR

Catherine Thrush is a creative powerhouse. She has worked as a glass artist, an illustrator, a web designer, a screenwriter, and a novelist. She wrote her first book, Quest of the Faes at the age of eighteen. It was published while she was in college working toward her studio art degree. Her screenplay and historical fiction manuscript, Lady Blade, have won several contests and led to her continuing work writing the Lady Blade series of novels.

Catherine took up fencing with Salle DeCesare in her twenties and has been studying it ever since.

She and her husband Thomas Thrush founded the company Urban Realms to sell books and products they've created related to RPG gaming— one of their favorite hobbies.

Originally from Wisconsin, Catherine and her husband Tom lived in California for many years, and now call Portugal home.

BOOKS IN THE LADY BLADE SERIES

Prologue – *Before the Blade*
Book One – *The Maestro's Daughter*
Book Two – *Lady Blade*
Additional Game – *Lady Blade's Jaguar Jungle*

OTHER BOOKS BY CATHERINE THRUSH

A New Look at Old Words
Quest of the Faes